Follow the bestselling adven... P9-CEF-398

HEIRS OF THE FORCE

The *New York Times* bestselling debut of the young Jedi Knights! Their training begins . . .

SHADOW ACADEMY

The dark side of the Force has a new training ground: the Shadow Academy!

THE LOST ONES

An old friend of the twins could be the perfect candidate for the Shadow Academy!

LIGHTSABERS

At last, the time has come for the young Jedi Knights to build their weapons . . .

DARKEST KNIGHT

The Dark Jedi student Zekk must face his old friends Jacen and Jaina—once and for all.

JEDI UNDER SIEGE

The final battle between Luke Skywalker's Jedi academy and the evil Shadow Academy . . .

And now, the Young Jedi Knights' adventures continue with

SHARDS OF ALDERAAN

This book also contains a special sneak preview of the next STAR WARS: YOUNG JEDI KNIGHTS adventure:

DIVERSITY ALLIANCE

ABOUT THE AUTHORS

KEVIN J. ANDERSON and his wife, **REBECCA MOESTA**, have been involved in many STAR WARS projects. Together, they are writing the eleven volumes of the YOUNG JEDI KNIGHTS saga for young adults, as well as creating the JUNIOR JEDI KNIGHTS series for younger readers. Rebecca Moesta is also writing the second trilogy of JUNIOR JEDI KNIGHTS adventures.

Kevin J. Anderson is the author of the STAR WARS: JEDI ACADEMY trilogy, the novel *Darksaber*, and the comic series THE SITH WAR and THE GOLDEN AGE OF THE SITH for Dark Horse comics. He has written many other novels, including two based on *The X-Files* television show. He has edited three STAR WARS anthologies: *Tales from the Mos Eisley Cantina*, in which Rebecca Moesta has a story; *Tales from Jabba's Palace*; and *Tales of the Bounty Hunters*.

STAR WARS
YOUNG JEDI KNIGHTS
SHARDS OF ALDERAAN

KEVIN J. ANDERSON
and REBECCA MOESTA

BOULEVARD BOOKS, NEW YORK

STAR WARS: YOUNG JEDI KNIGHTS
SHARDS OF ALDERAAN

A Boulevard Book / published by arrangement with
Lucasfilm Ltd.

PRINTING HISTORY
Boulevard edition / January 1997

The Putnam Berkley World Wide Web site address is
http://www.berkley.com/berkley

Make sure to check out *PB Plug*, the science
fiction/fantasy newsletter, at
http://www.pbplug.com

ISBN: 1-57297-207-6

BOULEVARD
Boulevard Books are published by The Berkley Publishing Group,
200 Madison Avenue, New York, New York 10016.
BOULEVARD and its logo are trademarks
belonging to Berkley Publishing Corporation.

PRINTED IN THE UNITED STATES OF AMERICA

10 9 8 7 6 5 4 3 2 1

To
Marina Fitch and Mark Budz—
colleagues, fellow dreamers, and friends

acknowledgments

Lillie E. Mitchell for her flying fingers, which continue to transcribe our dictation; Sue Rostoni at Lucasfilm for watching over all the details, in conjunction with Lucy Wilson and Allan Kausch, to keep these stories in line with other *Star Wars* adventures; Dave Dorman for his wonderful cover art, book after book after book; Mike Farnham for all the unexpected U-turns; Ginjer Buchanan and the folks at Berkley/Boulevard for their whole-hearted support and encouragement; Bill Smith and West End Games for background material; and Jonathan MacGregor Cowan for being our most avid and insistent test reader and brain-stormer.

STAR WARS

YOUNG JEDI KNIGHTS

WARS®

SHARDS OF ALDERAAN

MORNING MISTS CLUNG to the rubble of the Great Temple, making the huge stone blocks dangerously slippery as the repair crews set to work.

In the aftermath of the battle against the Shadow Academy, the jungle moon of Yavin 4 had been wounded and scarred. But now all of Luke Skywalker's new Jedi Knights worked together to heal . . . to rebuild.

Jaina Solo, already sore and sweaty from hours of hard work, climbed to the top of a fallen stone block and surveyed the wreckage around her. Surely the damage couldn't be as bad as it looked from here. . . .

The ancient temples had withstood the jungle's best efforts to tear them down for thousands of years. Two decades earlier, the Great Temple had served as a secret base during the Rebellion's initial struggles against the Empire. Years later, Jaina's uncle Luke had established his Jedi academy in the abandoned pyramid—making the small world a target for the remnants of the Empire once again.

Ancient as the temples were, the recent attacks by the Second Imperium and the Shadow Academy had been the most devastating the great monuments had ever suffered.

Although the battle had taken its toll, the survivors of Master Skywalker's academy worked day and night—not with despair, but hope. They had defeated the dark side of the Force. Now they had time to rebuild, to make everything stronger, because their enemy had been vanquished.

Halfway up the remains of the stair-stepped temple, cleanup crews climbed scaffolding made from saplings lashed together in a design Jaina herself had helped create. Clusters of Jedi students cleared battle debris from their headquarters while waiting for crews of New Republic engineers, architects, and laborers to arrive from Coruscant.

Tossing her head to keep her straight brown hair from getting in her eyes, Jaina stood watching for a moment with her hands on her narrow hips. She brushed a palm across her forehead to wipe away perspiration. Out in the surrounding jungles, other Jedi trainees hunted for shards of carved stone blasted from the Great Temple, cataloguing them so the pieces could be reassembled properly.

The task of rebuilding seemed enormous. Jaina found it hard to believe so much destruction could be caused by a single person. An Imperial commando had crept into the grand audience chamber during the height of battle, secretly planted his powerful explosives, and blown up the topmost levels of the Great Temple, killing himself in the process. Debris had pelted the battle-weary Jedi trainees, who had thought the day's devastation over.

Including Zekk, she thought with a pang.

The rain of shrapnel had seriously injured Jaina's friend-turned-enemy, Zekk, who had been threatening Jaina with his lightsaber at the time. Only after the blast did she realize that Zekk had actually *saved* her and the others . . . by preventing them from going into the temple he knew was doomed to explode.

Zekk had received medical attention at

Lando Calrissian's GemDiver Station, but had suffered a relapse on his return to Yavin 4. Jaina wondered if the dark-haired young man had simply been overwhelmed by the weight of his own gloom and guilt because of the evil work he had done for the Shadow Academy. Now he recovered in a restored room in the lower levels of the pyramid.

But Zekk had much to atone for, and he seemed intent on accepting the blame for all that had happened. . . .

Up on the scaffolding Jaina saw her Wookiee friend Lowbacca and Tenel Ka, the one-armed warrior girl from Dathomir, assisting each other in shoring up a high, unstable section of wall.

Near them, balanced precariously on a wooden shelf, worked Raynar Thul. The son of a former noble from Alderaan, the boy traditionally wore garish and colorful costumes—though at the moment his robes were dusty and dirty. It seemed that his recent ordeal had begun a change in him for the better. He had been utterly humiliated in the struggle against the Shadow Academy, thrown into the river mud and discarded as an incompetent foe. Since then, Raynar appeared more subdued and was doing his best to pitch in, as if he had become aware that perhaps he wasn't as important and talented as he had considered himself.

In the temple clearing a towering reptilian beast of burden moved about nervously. The ronto had been donated by a trader from Tatooine to assist the Jedi academy in its reconstruction efforts. The massive creature was skittish and difficult to handle at times, but its brute strength proved useful. Jaina watched the ronto tugging against ropes to move a huge block of stone into place beneath the main scaffolding supports.

She heard the shouts and calls of other Jedi trainees conferring as they bustled about. Their voices were clear in the misty air. The jungle itself seemed to watch in stunned silence as the Jedi academy tended its wounds and prepared to come back better than ever.

As the morning mist burned away and sunlight painted the forest floor, Jaina turned to see Luke Skywalker in his Jedi robe standing alone and motionless atop one of the tallest blocks. The sun shone directly into his clear blue eyes, but he didn't blink. The Jedi Master watched the complex activity intently as his trainees pulled together to rebuild.

The Jedi academy would be strong again; its future was wide open. Jaina knew that now, after the final defeat of its greatest enemy, the New Republic could at last enter a golden age of peace and prosperity.

The scaffolding creaked beneath Tenel Ka's bare feet, and she adjusted her balance, feeling her muscles ripple. Physical exercise always felt good, challenging, refreshing. Today she did not assume a fighting stance, but a careful acrobat's posture that allowed her to scramble along the narrow log platform to the wall's outermost stone blocks.

While some of the larger stones at the bottom of the rebuilt wall looked less stable, she knew her own layers of the reconstruction were solid. She had learned to pay careful attention to details, lest her own actions strike back at her. The sloppy and hurried construction of her first lightsaber caused it to explode during a practice session, and she had lost her arm. Now she knew mistakes could cost her life.

From above, Lowbacca grunted and reached down to haul up a pallet of stone adhesives that would cement the construction materials together. Moving with an easy grace, the lanky, ginger-furred Wookiee swung down from a carved rock ledge onto the scaffolding. He parted his lips and bared his teeth at Tenel Ka in a broad smile.

"Master Lowbacca, I do believe you're showing off," said Em Teedee, the miniaturized translating droid attached to Lowie's fiber belt. The Wookiee chuffed in amusement and dangled from the scaffolding, smearing the thick adhesive into a crack between two large blocks lower on the wall.

Still hanging, Lowie turned about to find himself eye to eye with the towering ronto. The giant beast blinked and snorted in surprise, then plodded away, leaving Lowie to wrinkle his black nose in distaste at its bad breath.

"Oh, my!" Em Teedee wailed. "If only my olfactory sensors could shut down! They must surely run the risk of overloading from that dreadful stench."

Tenel Ka offered Lowie her arm to help him back up.

Near the base of the wall, Raynar stood on the scaffolding in his colorful, dirt-smudged robes. The young man worked close to them, but still independently, not yet ready to become a full-fledged member of the team. He stretched out his hands and closed his eyes, concentrating as he attempted to use the Force to nudge the lower blocks into a more stable position.

Tenel Ka was pleased to see Raynar working to improve himself. In her experience of watching him, the overconfident Raynar had usually demonstrated more interest in his *importance* as a Jedi than in acquiring demonstrable Jedi skills.

In general, Tenel Ka herself chose not to use the Force if she could find any other way to solve her problems . . . though after her left arm had been severed, she had come to realize that *all* skills made up a person's resources, not just their physical or mental abilities.

Below, the ronto handlers yelled at the creature, which turned from one side to the other, shifting beneath its heavy load. Confused by conflicting directions, the beast swung its head, trying to move along opposing paths but unable to decide which way to go.

Tenel Ka froze, sensing the trouble a moment before it happened. Trumpeting in distress, the ronto twitched its tail in agi-

tation. The reptilian beast turned halfway
around and clumsily bumped into the scaffolding supports that ran along one of the
temple walls. Several Jedi trainees shouted
and scrambled for cover.

A load of stone blocks tumbled from
above as the vines holding a wooden pallet
snapped. The blocks crashed down, bang-
ing into supports and dislodging a small
keystone in the unstable portion of wall. As
a result, the entire structure began to
collapse.

Raynar stood right in the middle of the
impending avalanche.

"Lowbacca!" Tenel Ka cried—and the
Wookiee saw the boy's danger the moment
she did. She leaped out into open space,
somersaulting as the wall shuddered and
began to break apart.

Tenel Ka landed on a support strut right
beside Raynar. The boy whirled about,
sensing his peril but not knowing what to
do. Above her Tenel Ka saw Lowbacca
grasp one of the vines attached to the
scaffolding. He swung down, yowling a
primal battle challenge.

With only one arm Tenel Ka could not
grab Raynar and swing herself clear of the
falling rocks. Thinking quickly, she did the

next best thing: she tackled Raynar backward just as Lowie came careening down toward them. Still holding on to the vine, the Wookiee slammed into the brightly robed young man, scooped him up, and whisked him away.

As Lowbacca dove aside, rocks crashed, tumbled, fell. Tenel Ka lunged out of the way, sprang down to the next level, and swung herself to the ground. Then she leaped forward with all her might, just one step ahead of the crushing stone blocks. Though normally grim and serious, she let out an exhilarated cry that rose above the clatter of the collapsing wall. She heard Lowbacca roar in triumph, too, having landed safely with the other Jedi trainee.

Startled by the loud sound of the avalanche it had accidentally caused, the huge ronto reared and bellowed, snapping its last restraints. It lumbered off, crashing through the jungle as its handlers fled to avoid being trampled.

Trembling and panting from the exertion, her heart pounding in her ears, Tenel Ka watched with relief as the last stones pattered down. Lowie stayed close to Raynar, who huddled on the ground trying to regain his composure. The young man brushed off his robes and managed a shaky smile as other Jedi came running to make sure no one had been hurt.

Seeing two days' work collapsed around them, Tenel Ka shook her head. It was a disheartening sight . . . but merely a setback, not a disaster.

While the other Jedi trainees scrambled to straighten out the mess at the temple, Jacen Solo dashed into the jungle after the poor frightened ronto. He knew no one else would do it, and he was the best person for the job. Jacen had a knack for sensing animals and communicating with them.

The clumsy beast was naturally skittish, so it was hardly surprising that the loud roar of the stone wall collapsing had spooked it. The ronto had been taken from its dry desert world and brought to a frighteningly dense jungle to work in a place with strange smells, strange sounds, strange predators.

"Come here, ronto," Jacen coaxed. Although he didn't know the creature's name, he knew that most animals could recognize a kind, understanding voice. "Come here, boy—it's okay."

The reptilian beast had plowed a wide

swath through the underbrush, knocking branches aside, crushing weeds, uprooting vines. Jacen stepped over a broken tree trunk and waded through mashed bushes, sidestepping the deep footprints squished into the moist ground. The ronto's trail certainly wasn't difficult to follow!

He crept forward, sending out soothing thoughts . . . though he doubted the distressed ronto could sense him yet. Jacen knew the creature had a kind disposition and sincerely wanted to help, though it didn't seem to comprehend its handlers' instructions most of the time.

After nearly an hour, Jacen spotted the huge beast and approached it quietly. It had stumbled into a thicket and now stood trembling and exhausted, its sides heaving. Rows of peglike teeth glinted as the ronto opened and closed its mouth. Rivers of drool poured down onto the lush weeds. The creature's leathery hide rippled as it shivered with fear.

"It's all right. Good boy," Jacen said, creeping closer.

The ronto turned its huge crested head, its giant eyes rolling. . . . Jacen approached with calm confidence, sending soothing thoughts. The creature could probably bite off his head with one snap of its jaws, but Jacen knew the ronto wouldn't do that. He knew it meant no harm.

The beast had been frightened by the accident, and Jacen sensed the dim fear that it would be punished for its clumsiness. But Jacen cooed, easing forward. "Hey, want to hear a joke? Um . . . why did the ronto run into the jungle?" He took another step. "Uh, I don't know—I haven't thought of a punch line yet. Got any ideas?"

The ronto eyed him warily and then, sensing that Jacen was a friend after all, suddenly became cheerful again, eager to please. It bent down and snorted.

"It's all right," Jacen said again. "We still want your help. You haven't been bad. It was just an accident. You do great work." He could feel the ronto's happiness as he gave it that small nugget of appreciation. "You're very strong."

Finally reaching its side, Jacen stroked a rough leathery flank. The ronto leaned down to sniff him. He patted the beast's head crest. "Would you like to help us?" he said. "Do you want to work? We'd really like that. It's very important work."

Jacen sensed understanding going off

like fireworks in the creature's mind, and he was almost overwhelmed by the exuberance.

Work, work, work, work!

The ronto *wanted* to be useful, *wanted* to show its strength and its willingness to help out. It *liked* to haul objects for its masters. But it had been confused by complicated tasks and too many strangers giving too many instructions all at once.

"It's okay," Jacen said. "We'll give you some good work to do, and we'll be happy to have your help."

The ronto flared its head crest, and Jacen decided he could take the creature back to the Great Temple now—but it was a long walk. Silently asking its permission, he climbed up onto the beast's back. *Why not ride in style?*

The ronto seemed utterly delighted to be put into service for such a task, and pranced proudly back through the jungle toward the Great Temple.

2

A COLD BLACKNESS surrounded Zekk, like the impenetrable depths of a forest in which he had lost his way. Like deep space, endless and dark. . . .

Though immersed in frigid shadows, his body burned with fever. He didn't know where he was. Drenched with perspiration, Zekk longed for a cool breeze, or at least the comfort of darkness.

But the darkness held no real comfort, no peace. He knew that now. He had been so easily fooled.

A red beam, bright as a laser, stabbed his eyes, illuminating a dream jungle around him. No path led through the tangle of undergrowth. No way out. . . . With detached curiosity, Zekk noticed that the bright red glow sprang from a hilt clutched in his own hand. Had he been holding a lightsaber all along? Perhaps he could use his scarlet blade to carve a way out of this nightmare.

Moving numbly, Zekk stepped forward, raising the weapon that burned as brightly as his fever. Cool drafts of hope sang through his veins like the hum of his pulsating lightsaber.

But before Zekk could slice through the foliage in front of him, a slender tree transformed itself into an ominous figure—a woman with violet eyes and a spine-shouldered cape. Tangled vines became flowing hair as black as the garment she wore, and Tamith Kai's wine-dark lips twisted in a sneer.

"Poor young fool," she said. The Nightsister's deep, rich voice mocked him. "Did you really think you could leave us, abandon our teachings? It was your own choice to come to the dark side in the first place."

Zekk threw his shoulders back. He would not fear Tamith Kai. She could be defeated. She *had been* defeated. The Nightsister had been killed in the attack on the Jedi academy when her battle platform had crashed in flames into the wide river near the Massassi temples.

"It was my choice, yes. But now I *choose*

to go," Zekk said, stepping forward to make a path.

The Nightsister's laugh was harsh. "Fool! Your choices are much more limited than you believe."

She had no hold over him, Zekk reminded himself. He had not liked or admired her in life, and now that the Nightsister was dead, how could she hold him back? He swung the bright blade in a wide arc toward the trees. Tamith Kai's image blurred like a faulty hologram and dissolved.

A searing wave of darkness washed across Zekk's vision. After it swept past, a new and more terrifying image stood before Zekk: Brakiss, the Master of the Shadow Academy.

His mentor.

Stern eyes gazed out from a serene, sculpture-perfect face in its frame of pale hair. Silvery robes rippled as Brakiss spread his arms. "How can you leave now, Zekk? After all I've taught you? *You* are my darkest knight." A subtly powerful tone colored the evil Jedi Master's words, a tone of disappointment . . . of betrayal.

Zekk took a step backward. Feverish heat flared inside him, threatening to consume him. Rivers of perspiration ran down his forehead, his neck. Zekk shook his head, sending a rain of hot droplets flying out from his long, dark hair. "I'm sorry, Master Brakiss, but you were wrong. The dark side couldn't save you, or the Second Imperium—or me."

"Don't throw it all away, Zekk. Consider how much you still could learn from the dark side," Brakiss said, his voice compelling, urgent.

The scorching heat inside Zekk became so intense that waves radiated from him, shimmering in the air and blurring Brakiss's face. "No," Zekk whispered, feeling the furnace blast of his own breath. In the distance, a trickling sound tortured him with the promise of cooling relief. If only the rain could get through the dense tangle of branches to refresh him.

"If you truly think I am wrong, Zekk, then strike me down," Brakiss said. His voice was cool, silky. "Isn't that what the light side would want you to do . . . to prove your loyalty, your commitment?"

Zekk wavered. Could it be true? Was that his only way out?

No, that way led to the dark side. There must be another way.

Suddenly, locking his lightsaber in the

ON position, Zekk hurled the scarlet blade upward with all the strength in his feverish body.

The blade spun as it sailed higher and higher, slicing through leaves and branches on its way. The image of Brakiss disappeared in the shower of leaves, bark, and twigs that fluttered down around Zekk.

Still the lightsaber spun higher, all the way up until it pierced the canopy of the dark jungle. The outside rain came pouring down. Zekk had just enough time to feel the patter of cool droplets on his burning skin before a tumbling branch struck his head and a corona of brightness burst behind his emerald-green eyes. . . .

Zekk woke to the sound of trickling water. Was it still the dream rain? He could feel the dampness of cool moisture against his skin, and a shaft of bright sunlight lay across his face. He opened his eyes—and found himself in a strange room with thick, ancient-looking stone walls. The sunlight poured through a deep window slit in one wall. But where was the trickling sound coming from?

"Water," he said in a hoarse croak.

"Hey, you're awake," a familiar-sounding voice exclaimed. The grinning face of Jacen Solo appeared beside Zekk. "Did you ask for water? I've got some right here." He pressed a cup to Zekk's lips, and Zekk swallowed gratefully.

"Jaina put in the wall-fountain while you were unconscious," Jacen explained. "This room didn't have running water, and she thought you might need it."

"Unconscious?" Zekk tried to push himself up to a sitting position. "How long?"

"Whoa there," Jacen said, propping a cushion behind Zekk and pushing the young man back onto it. "Better not rush things, or you might have another relapse."

Zekk found his head swimming and subsided onto the cushion. "*Another* relapse? Jacen, where have I been?"

"You gave us all a pretty big scare, you know," Jacen said. "We thought you were just fine after a day or two in the bacta tank on GemDiver Station, but when we got back here to Yavin 4, you collapsed. You've been in a coma for days now. Uncle Luke says there are some injuries a bacta tank just can't heal." Jacen's brows drew together over his brandy-brown eyes, and he ran a hand through his tousled curls. "Blaster bolts, for a while there we weren't sure you were going to make it."

The words brought an image flashing through Zekk's mind from the Shadow Academy's final battle with the Jedi academy: the *Lightning Rod* trailing smoke and flames. "Peckhum?" he asked.

"Right over there." Jacen pointed to a corner of the room, where the old spacer sat dozing in a chair, grizzled chin propped on one fist. "Hasn't left your side since the day you collapsed. Want me to wake him up?"

Zekk shook his head, a motion that made his temples throb. It was enough to know that his old friend was still alive and well. "Let him sleep," he rasped, then took another drink of cool, delicious water.

"I think you're really going to like it here at the Jedi academy, Zekk," Jacen said. "Uncle Luke says you can stay and train with us, if you want to. We've all taken turns tending you: Jaina, Lowie—even Tenel Ka. Of course, she's not quite sure she trusts you yet, but I think she'll come around. I've been bringing my stump lizard along with me when I watch you. He and his mate found their way back to me after the explosion—I think they hid down in the hangar bay—so they must have good luck. Hey, I can't wait to tell everybody that you're awake and feeling better. D'you think you could eat if I brought you some food?"

Zekk nodded uncertainly.

"Great, I'll go get you something," Jacen said. "And that reminds me of a joke. I'll tell it to you when I get back. Can you watch my stump lizard for me for a few minutes while I'm gone? Everything's going to be just fine now, Zekk. You'll see." With that Jacen dashed out the door, leaving Zekk to stare after him wondering.

But he wasn't at all convinced that everything would be "just fine." Ever again.

3

A SOFT RAIN fell outside the Jedi academy, so gentle that Tenel Ka hardly noticed it. Clothed only in her lizard hide outfit, she had long ago trained her body to endure variations in her environment, refusing to let anything distract her from important matters. Focused on restoring the damaged practice courtyard beside the Great Temple, the warrior girl moved swiftly about her tasks.

Even without her left arm, Tenel Ka never assumed she should do less work than the others. The need to pull her own weight was too much a part of her personality for her to consider anything else. Tenel Ka acknowledged that her pride had been a major cause of the lightsaber accident, and she had come to view the loss of her arm as a test of her mettle, a challenge to her persistence.

Tenel Ka had been an excellent gymnast,

swimmer, and climber when she'd had both hands, and now she refused to let her missing limb stop her from doing the things she enjoyed. That meant she had to find alternative approaches and solutions. Her friends understood this; Lowbacca, the twins, and sometimes even their little brother Anakin worked at finding novel ways to help her overcome various obstacles.

Strangely, these small victories had become a source of secret enjoyment for her. Whenever a situation arose that normally required the use of two arms, Tenel Ka challenged herself to find another way to accomplish the task—such as resetting some of these flagstones in the practice courtyard.

Clearing the debris from the explosion had been a fairly simple matter. Other Jedi students had helped, using the Force to remove broken rubble and chunks of vine-covered stone. One group had used the enthusiastic ronto to haul heavy fallen blocks away from the opening of the hangar bay.

Putting the pieces back together, however, proved to be much more complex.

Tenel Ka caught a flash of color out of the corner of her eye and noted Raynar striding up. The young man set to work near her, his spiky blond hair damp and his robes drooping in the misty rains. The usually haughty teen was trying to maneuver a flagstone into place with his foot to avoid getting more mud on his purple, orange, red, and yellow clothes.

Tenel Ka had noticed that ever since the Shadow Academy's attack, Raynar had found reasons to stay near the four young Jedi Knights. Though his bearing remained proud, the young man worked hard and willingly.

Tenel Ka pounded her flagstone firmly into place and filled in the surrounding cracks with packed dirt and mud. Then she helped Raynar rotate his stone so that it fit better beside hers. The two of them remained quiet, intent on their tasks.

Jaina and Lowbacca continued rebuilding the adjacent courtyard wall. "You know, I think repairs on your T-23 are coming along pretty well, Lowie," Jaina said. "Maybe we can tinker with it again this afternoon after I finish my shift watching Zekk."

Lowbacca barked his agreement. "An excellent idea, Mistress Jaina," Em Teedee chimed in. "With my new set of diagnostic subroutines, we ought to have that skyhopper fully operational again in very little time."

"This is a fact," Tenel Ka said, standing up. "I will be happy to assist you. Your brother will no doubt offer to provide entertainment."

"I don't know . . . I think one of us still needs to stay with Zekk," Jaina said doubtfully, "even if he's still unconscious."

"Then again, maybe not," Jacen's voice came from the opposite side of the wall. Tenel Ka turned to see the young Jedi appear, stepping over a low pile of rubble in the broken wall and flashing a wide grin. "Hey, good news—Zekk's out of his coma. Everything's going to be just fine now."

"Well, what are we waiting for?" Jaina asked, brushing herself off. Her cheeks, damp from the mist, flushed pink with excitement. "Come on. Let's go see him."

"Whoa!" Jacen said, holding up his hands. "I just got him some soup. Old Peckhum fed it to him, and after they talked for a few minutes Zekk fell asleep again. I think we'd better let him rest for a while."

"Okay," Jaina agreed, looking disappointed though greatly relieved now that her friend seemed to be out of danger.

From his place on the second level outside the broken pyramid, Master Skywalker called for his students to assemble so that he could speak with them. The Jedi trainees gathered and watched their teacher with great interest. A hush as light as the falling mist fell over the group.

"It's an unusual experience for us to meet out in the open like this, but new experiences, even painful ones, can be good," Master Skywalker said. "They help us grow. We must learn the lessons each experience offers us, and then move forward."

Tenel Ka nodded, thinking of all the ways she had had to adapt after her accident.

"The galaxy does not stay the same. It changes from day to day, and we must change and grow to meet new challenges." Master Skywalker continued. "As Jedi, we must never allow ourselves to become stagnant or self-satisfied. We must be ever vigilant, aware of what is happening around us, and ready to adapt to changing circumstances." He glided down the temple steps and walked among the students, stopping near Lowbacca and Jaina.

"We are surrounded by examples of adaptation and change. Take Lowbacca's translating droid, for instance. Em Teedee's primary purpose has been to translate Wookiee speech into Basic. But now that some of you can understand part of Lowie's words, that skill is no longer so essential. Em Teedee requested additional programming to help him adapt to the new situation, and so Jaina and Lowie have been enriching Em Teedee's subroutines, and even adding new language skills."

The little droid's optical sensors glowed with pleasure at being singled out.

"All of us need to do the same thing," the Jedi Master continued. Suddenly he paused and cocked his head, as if listening.

Jaina whirled to look at the landing field in front of the Great Temple. "Dad?" she whispered, her face filled with an expression of surprise and disbelief.

A murmur went up from the Jedi trainees, and Tenel Ka turned to see the *Millennium Falcon* making its final approach through the cloudy skies of the jungle moon.

"I think that will be all for now," Master Skywalker said in a concerned voice. "Please return to your activities while I welcome our unexpected guests."

At the teacher's dismissal, Jacen and

Jaina took off for the landing field at a run, with Lowbacca and Tenel Ka following close behind.

At first Jaina was too stunned to speak when Han Solo swept her up in a quick hug, then repeated the process with Jacen. Lowie and his tall uncle Chewbacca exchanged happy roars.

Chewie tossed the twins high into the air by turns and caught them again, as if they were mere babies, while Han put a hand on Luke's shoulder and began talking in a low, urgent voice. Jaina finally managed to ask her father what he was doing there. She was almost afraid of the answer, since they had been through so many changes, had heard so much bad news recently.

"Hey, you wouldn't want your old dad to become predictable, would you?" Han said, flashing a roguish grin. "I've got a few surprises left in me. Just finished a trip to GemDiver Station to see Lando on my way back from an important trade conference. When your mom got some disturbing news, she thought it'd be best if I stopped by to deliver it in person."

Imagining the worst, Jaina felt the blood drain from her face. "What is it, Dad?

What's happened?" In her heart, she feared that it was something else to do with Zekk, some other dark thing he had done.

Han's face looked grim. "I need to talk to a student named Raynar Thul. Do you know him?"

"Of course we *know* him . . . ," Jacen said.

All of a sudden, as if from nowhere, the boy himself appeared out of the mist beside Jaina. He had followed the young Jedi Knights in their rush to the damp landing field.

"I am Raynar Thul. You may address me directly."

Looking at the blond-haired boy, Han sighed. "I'm sorry, kid, but I've got some rough news. I'm afraid your father's disappeared. No one's heard from him for several days."

Raynar's normally rosy complexion paled. "My father is too important a man, a former noble of Alderaan. He can't just disappear. There must be some mistake."

Han gave Raynar a sympathetic look. "Afraid not, kid. Your father and I have been serving on the New Republic Trade Council together. We were supposed to meet at a major conference on Shumavar, but he never showed."

Raynar swallowed hard as Han Solo continued quickly. "'Bout a week ago your father told me he was starting trade negotiations with a Twi'lek woman, Nolaa Tarkona, who's heading some new political movement. He was supposed to finalize the details with her during the Shumavar conference. Wasn't sure why, but I smelled something rotten in the deal. Tried to warn your father, but he wouldn't listen to me."

Raynar's cheeks flushed deep red. "Bornan Thul *always* listens to sound advice."

Han shrugged. "Well, I guess he wasn't too impressed by the advice of a former smuggler who managed to marry well. At any rate, your father never arrived at the trade conference. Your mother contacted us on Coruscant a few days ago, said your father disappeared without a word. His brother hasn't heard from him either. Has your dad tried to contact you at all?"

Raynar shook his head, then raised his chin. His eyes flashed. "Has a proper team been organized to look for him? We should begin a search immediately. I'll lead it myself, if need be. I could—"

"Just a minute there, kid," Han said,

holding his palms out. "I got strict orders from your family to make sure you stay here with Luke. That's the best protection I can imagine. If your father's been kidnapped by some unsavory types, your mother and your uncle don't want you out in the middle of things. We sure don't want to have to track *you* down and rescue *you*, too. Best thing you can do for the moment is to lay low and let us do the looking."

Feeling a rush of sympathy for Raynar, Jaina put a hand on the young man's arm. "I'm sure it'll be all right, Raynar," she said.

Raynar threw back his shoulders and sent Jaina a frightened look that he tried to mask with disdain. "Of course it will be all right," he said. "My father's an important man." He looked back at Han Solo.

"Very well then. I'll stay on Yavin 4. Just see to it that you have competent searchers looking for my father."

4

SPACE WAS VAST, an infinite pool in all directions . . . whether up and out of the galactic plane, or deeper inward toward the Core Systems. The galaxy held countless hiding places: planets, asteroid fields, star clusters, gas clouds . . . even these empty wastelands without stars.

It would take the best of bounty hunters to find any quarry under such circumstances.

And Boba Fett was the best.

He cruised through the wilderness between star systems, all sensors alert, scanning for any sign of his prey. He had dropped out of hyperspace in his ship, the *Slave IV*, just long enough to take data. On this stop, his sensitive detectors picked up no energy readings, no sign of any ship's passage within half a parsec. Nothing had crossed this empty no-man's-land in the past decade.

Grim and persistent, Boba Fett studied readings through the narrow T-slit in his Mandalorian helmet. He nodded, but spoke no word into the flight recorder. Bornan Thul was not here. He would have to search elsewhere. The hunt might be long, but in the end no one could elude Boba Fett. No one.

He clutched the *Slave IV*'s modified controls—propulsion systems, navigational computers, and acceleration foils that were illegal in many systems. But Fett paid no attention to legalities. Mere laws did not apply to him. He obeyed his own code of ethics and morality: the Bounty Hunter's Creed.

Launching his ship into hyperspace again, Fett replayed the holomessage Nolaa Tarkona had sent to him. His assignment for this hunt. Perhaps he might find other clues there. He already knew the message by heart, had listened to it eight times on his journey, but he studied it once more anyway.

Boba Fett carefully observed the female Twi'lek's face: the folds around her pinkish eyes, the greenish cast of her skin, her pointed white teeth. Nolaa Tarkona's one green-skinned head-tail dangled from the back of her skull and curled around her shoulders. Her voice was deep and melodious, not the dry, crisp hiss he might have expected from a surreptitious crime lord. Tarkona led a growing political movement known as the Diversity Alliance. Nothing overtly criminal . . . at least not yet.

Boba Fett did not care about his employer's politics or her reasons. That was not a bounty hunter's business. She had set the bounty, and Fett had a job to do.

The hologram spoke. "Boba Fett, your fame has spanned decades and crossed the galaxy—now I offer you the greatest assignment of your career." The Twi'lek woman stroked her head-tail. Her eyes looked like disks of rose quartz glowing with internal fire.

"Find the man named Bornan Thul, an important trade commissioner from Coruscant. He was a member of the nobility on Alderaan before that planet was destroyed, and he has become a trade negotiator in the New Republic government. I sent him as my intermediary to procure a valuable cargo containing certain information crucial to the Diversity Alliance. He was to deliver that shipment to me at the Shumavar trade conference, where I was scheduled to give a speech. But his ship vanished en route—and my information disappeared with him. Find Bornan Thul. I *must* have that cargo."

She leaned forward, her mouth opened in a smile that showed off her jagged teeth. "When Darth Vader hired you to find Han Solo, the bounty was quite substantial. I will pay you *twice* that if you find Bornan Thul and bring me my cargo. A few other bounty hunters will be searching as well—but you are the *best*, Boba Fett. I expect results from you."

Inside his cramped cockpit, Boba Fett switched off the holoprojector and swept his gloved hands through the dissolving sparkles of color as the three-dimensional image faded. "You will *have* results," he muttered, his voice loud and raspy in the oppressively silent ship. . . .

Approaching another solar system in which there were no catalogued planets capable of supporting life, Fett dropped out of hyperspace to continue his search. His navicomputer had a map of all star systems in the sector where the trade negotiator had vanished. His data banks were crammed with unusual information and reports, any bit of which might give him a clue that would lead to the discovery of his prey.

Bornan Thul had flown alone in his ship, refusing the standard diplomatic escort to which he was entitled. Secretly checking through New Republic flight records, Fett saw that this was quite an unusual request for Thul. The former Alderaan noble, a fair pilot at best, preferred large escorts and excessive pomp and ceremony. Flying off alone in a supply cruiser seemed highly uncharacteristic for this man.

Fett wondered if Thul had discovered something unusual about the nature of his cargo, or its importance to the Twi'lek political leader's movement. Boba Fett himself did not know what information the cargo contained. He had only to find it and return it to Nolaa Tarkona.

Fett approached the bleak, uninhabited system—a small double star with three frozen gas planets in distant orbits and two rocky inner planets. After a few moments of scanning, the *Slave IV*'s sophisticated sensors detected processed metal, faint lubricants, traces of stardrive fuel, and spin-sealed Tibanna gas—a strong enough reading to indicate a whole ship. The source seemed to be located inside the ragged strands of a rocky ring that surrounded the outermost gas planet.

Boba Fett nodded in respect. A good place to hide, and a good system in which to remain hidden. With a bright flare of its sublight engines, the *Slave IV* homed in on the sensor signal.

Fett had studied the history and family of Bornan Thul, hoping for clues. Understanding his prey was the best way to catch it. The Alderaan noble had a wife, Aryn, who remained under heavy security on her own fleet of trade ships . . . a brother, Tyko, who kept himself heavily guarded in his administration facilities on the droid-manufacturing world of Mechis III . . . and one heir, his son. The young man, Raynar, had attended the best schools, studied under the most efficient tutors, and was now enrolled in Skywalker's Jedi academy. Obviously, Bornan Thul doted on his son and gave the boy everything he desired, with the result that he had worked for nothing in his life.

In fact, Raynar Thul might make a good hostage—if it came to that.

But perhaps it would all end here at this out-of-the-way planet.

Most of Fett's detector readings were indistinct and scattered due to ionization and outgassing from the broken rocks and ice chunks in the planetary ring. Thul's ship might have crashed into some ring debris, scattering wreckage in a broad swath. A low, growling sound came from deep within Boba Fett's throat. The bounty would be cut in half if he found nothing but the wreckage of Thul's ship. The Twi'lek woman cared only about recovering the information from its cargo.

Fett looked out the *Slave IV*'s cockpit windowport as he cruised into the swirling strip of rocky debris around the blue and white ice world. Following the sensor signal, he pulled up close to several long chunks of scattered metal: hull plating, blast shields from a space vessel—unmistakably, wreckage from a ship. Recent wreckage.

Fett ran a quick analysis and determined that the hull plating matched that of the type of vehicle Thul had been using. He allowed himself a grunt of disappointment. Perhaps everything had been destroyed, cargo and all, leaving only this debris.

But if that were true, Fett realized, there should have been more mass . . . much more. His sensors had picked up a signal strong enough to account for an entire ship, and this debris amounted to no more than a hundred kilograms or so. He wondered where the rest could have gone. Maybe the cargo and its "crucial" information remained intact after all—

He reacted with lightning speed as the attacking vessel came around a frozen methane asteroid. Another bounty hunter ship, shaped like a deadly pinwheel star, its laser cannons already taking aim!

Boba Fett sent *Slave IV* into a spin, twirling away from four rapid-fire laser bolts. The ambushing bounty hunter did not continue to shoot his lasers, powering up an ion cannon instead—which was exactly what Fett would have done. An ion cannon blast would neutralize all power systems on his ship, leaving him dead in space, where his enemy could dissect him at will and strip away his possessions and weapons.

A bounty hunter, a good bounty hunter, always attempted to make efficient use of resources.

Fett's weapons systems were not engaged. He mentally cursed himself for not having considered the danger while he'd approached the suspicious debris. If he continued to be so foolish, he deserved to die!

This fighter had been lying in wait for him. Perhaps the other bounty hunter had found the debris himself, or perhaps he had actually placed it there as a lure. Or perhaps the enemy had destroyed Bornan Thul's ship.

As Boba Fett zipped and dodged, the attacker came on, clearly holding the upper hand. Fett tried to accelerate, ducking in and around the rocks of the planetary ring, but he knew that was merely a delaying tactic. He had no chance of evading pursuit when his attacker was this close.

A message came over his comm system. "Boba Fett, I recognize your ship. This is Moorlu—the bounty hunter who's going to destroy you." The enemy chuckled, a low phlegmy laugh. "I will display your helmet as my trophy!"

"I'm not a trophy yet," Fett muttered. Planning the best way to defeat his overconfident opponent, he took a desperate gamble.

Boba Fett allowed himself to be hit.

The ion blast rippled against the *Slave IV*'s hull, frying his electrical systems, leaving him dead in space, so that he drifted around the gaseous planet, apparently helpless.

Apparently.

"Got you, Boba Fett! Now I can take care of you, steal everything you own—and use it to chase down Bornan Thul."

Moorlu, you talk too much, Fett thought, as the comm system shut down.

Dangling in the arms of zero gravity, without ship's power, he waited as the other bounty hunter's pinwheel ship approached like a spider-rat to disassemble its prey.

Moorlu didn't notice the pneumatic launcher mounted at the rear weapons hatch of *Slave IV*.

Boba Fett cranked the launcher by hand, using mechanical systems only. He waited patiently to take his only chance. At least the comm system had shut down, so he didn't have to listen to Moorlu's obnoxious gloating.

When the ambushing bounty hunter's ship came close enough for a ballistic launch, Fett aimed by sight and triggered the spring release. A torpedo dart filled with concussion explosives flew across space as if spat from a slingshot.

Boba Fett's aim was true.

The high explosives penetrated Moorlu's hull, ripping out the fuel pods beneath the pinwheel engines, setting up a detonation that left Moorlu dead in space. *Literally* dead in space.

Fett despised bounty hunters that were too easy to kill, but he supposed it cleared the playing field of amateurs. . . .

It took Boba Fett four standard hours to realign his electrical systems, power them up again, and purge the bad signals from his memory banks. Moorlu's ion cannon had done significant, but not irreparable damage.

Finally able to get down to the business of searching for his real quarry, Fett returned to the scraps of hull metal he had found earlier. He used a tractor beam to haul the shrapnel into his cargo bay, then carefully analyzed the burned edges and each outer surface. Surprisingly, the scrap hull plates contained a sequence of identifying serial numbers, enough to prove that this debris had unquestionably come from Bornan Thul's ship.

But he still couldn't find enough wreckage to account for the entire craft. If the vessel had exploded here, there should have been more debris.

No, the amount and the placement of the debris seemed too convenient, too calculated, too easy. He had found only one large piece of metal—and it *just happened* to contain a crucial serial number? Yes . . . convenient.

Fett analyzed again and found that all the scraps had been carefully removed. Nothing was vital. An engine cowling could easily be replaced, and the bits of exterior hull had no doubt been stripped away from a portion of the vessel that already had double plating, or from some area that could afford to be weakened.

Fett stood up from the pitted pieces of hull metal. Bornan Thul had planted this debris here on purpose, hoping to convince pursuers that his ship had been destroyed in the planetary rim. . . . If the ruse had been successful, Nolaa Tarkona would have had no choice but to believe her cargo lost and call off the entire bounty hunt.

Boba Fett crawled forward into the

cockpit, quite pleased with himself for unraveling the ruse. This Bornan Thul was proving to be a much more challenging quarry than he had anticipated.

He would enjoy hunting the man down.

5

JAINA STARED PENSIVELY at the wide, greenish-brown river that flowed past the Great Temple. Her boots sank into the soft, dark mud of the riverbank. In his defeat and despair at the end of the battle with the Shadow Academy, Zekk had covered himself with that mud, as if it could hide him from what he had done.

The sunlight that had burned away the earlier mist poured down onto the water and reflected back into the air, drenching the jungle with vibrant greens, blues, purples, and browns. Insects swarmed about, humming, buzzing, reveling in the change of weather.

Jaina wasn't sure what had drawn her here, but after visiting Zekk's room for the third time in as many hours, only to find him still asleep, she had decided to take a walk alone, hoping to sort out her thoughts.

She felt something unsettling in the atmosphere, and she didn't know what it was—or perhaps she did. Everything seemed different to her somehow. Familiar, yet different. Since the attack by the Second Imperium, the Jedi academy had changed.

Jaina made her way across stepping-stones in the river shallows to a broad, flat rock. Sitting down on it, she dangled the soles of her boots in the warm water, letting the strong current carry away the caked mud.

Why was change so difficult to accept, even when the changes were supposedly for the good? The academy felt different. Her studies felt different. Jedi trainees no longer spent their days in quiet contemplation and individual exercises; they had too much work to do repairing the damage from the recent battle—the conflict of Jedi against Jedi. Though Luke Skywalker's trainees had won, the Shadow Academy had shown them their vulnerabilities, their weaknesses. Nothing would ever be the same.

Even the Great Temple was different, many of its ancient blocks shattered in the explosion. Under the direction of her uncle Luke, the pyramid would be rebuilt, of course. But it could never be the *same* again.

Was that *bad*, though?

After all, the Jedi academy's greatest outside threat had been vanquished. The Shadow Academy station was gone forever, destroyed in orbit by its own implanted explosive systems. Yet, in an odd way this disturbed Jaina. She had found something comforting in *knowing* who the enemy was.

Brakiss and the Second Imperium were no longer a threat, and her friend Zekk had come back from the darkness. They could be together again, to face whatever the future held. So why wasn't she happy?

Jaina wasn't prepared to handle so many changes at once. Why couldn't things go back to the way they *were*? She was certain she still wanted to become a Jedi Knight, but it no longer seemed the only thing to do, the only possible path for her life. It no longer seemed like a simple choice. In fact, life seemed more complicated than ever before.

She leaned down and plucked a few pebbles from the shallow water, then tossed them one by one toward the center of the river. In seconds the strong current erased all ripples, all signs of the pebble's splash. Jaina bit her lower lip. In the end, was that all the effect her life would have? She wanted to do something *significant*, not disappear without a trace.

Jaina gazed down into the murky river, but she could see no farther into its depths than she could into the future. She tossed a larger rock this time, making a bigger splash, but with the same short-lived result.

Suddenly, a small flat stone skittered across the surface, bouncing past her as easily as sunlight skipping across the ripples, before disappearing toward the far shore.

Jaina turned and saw a dark-haired young man standing ankle-deep in water at the edge of the river. "Zekk!"

"Is this a private game, or can anyone play?" he asked, giving her a wan smile. He seemed barely able to stand.

"You look . . ." She paused, at a loss for words. His long hair, a shade lighter than black, contrasted starkly with the pale skin of his face. Purplish smudges beneath his emerald-green eyes made them look sunken and haunted. He looked as if he had not eaten for a week. "Uh, you look . . ."

"Alive?" Zekk suggested, smiling faintly.

Jaina cocked her head and looked him over, raising her eyebrows. "Well . . . just barely."

"I must be a pretty awful sight," Zekk said. "I actually feel better than I look. By a little bit, at least."

Jaina chuckled, feeling dizzy and tongue-tied. "Well, that's a relief." Somehow, she couldn't think of what to say to the friend who had once been so close. "Uh, do you need to sit down or anything?" She indicated a spot on the rock beside her.

Zekk shook his head. "I'm a bit shaky after so much time lying in bed, but I feel restless. I thought maybe we could take a walk in the jungle?" He spoke hesitantly, as if afraid she might reject his offer. "Together?"

Jaina slid off the flat stone and sloshed over to where he stood in the shallows. "Well, then," she said with a grin, "what are we *wading* for?"

Zekk groaned at the joke. "I think your twin brother is having a bad influence on you."

Jaina spent the next hour with Zekk. Trudging through the undergrowth, they made their own path. The two of them kept the conversation light, neutral, wandering along the borders of uncharted territories in their friendship. They crossed the river and made their way through the jungle to the ruins of the shield generator station. Mangled equipment and chunks of blasted plasteel still lay everywhere.

"Looks like those commandos did a pretty thorough job," Zekk said in a quiet voice. Jaina tried to determine if his statement held any pride that the Imperials, ostensibly under his command, had succeeded in their mission. But he sounded only tired and disappointed.

Jaina bit her lower lip. "Not much left here to salvage," she agreed. "Mom's sending an all new generator, state-of-the-art. New Republic engineers already cleared a fresh site for it right over there," she said, pointing toward another clearing just visible through the trees. "She's even going to station a military guardian force in orbit and upgrade all of our communications equipment. Uncle Luke doesn't like all these complications, but the Jedi academy will never be caught unguarded again."

Zekk nodded. "Master Brakiss and I—" His voice broke, but he cleared his throat and began again. "We always thought your defenses here were pitifully weak. It was stupid—naive at best—to leave Yavin 4 so unprotected. We thought it would be Master Skywalker's downfall."

Jaina swallowed hard. "It almost was. He was confident in the abilities of his trainees."

They stood in awkward silence for some moments. Zekk seemed old to Jaina now, much older than his years. Not on the outside, but inside—as if the darkness had stolen his innocence, charred his heart.

"Feels strange," she said at last, "all these changes around us."

A dark eyebrow raised above an emerald-green eye. "All these new defenses being added, you mean? In a way, it's making this place more like the Shadow Academy."

That wasn't what she had meant, but Jaina wasn't sure how to say it. "Zekk, do you remember the time on Coruscant when we slipped out in the middle of the night and went swimming in the fountain in Dhalbreth Square?"

A distant smile curved the corners of his mouth. "And the glowfish we disturbed made so much light that the New Republic security forces came running after us." He took a deep breath. "Of course I remember."

"I wish we could be like that again, back in those days, without everything that happened . . . afterward." Before he could comment, Jaina rushed on. "Zekk, if you stay here at the Jedi academy, Uncle Luke can teach you the right way to use the Force. We could have adventures together again, you and I—and Jacen and Lowie and Tenel Ka. We're thinking about going to the Alderaan system to get a gift for my mother's birthday. A memento of her home from the asteroid field there. You could come with us."

"I wish I could just go home . . . ," Zekk murmured thoughtfully.

"When we get back from Alderaan you could start your training. A fresh start."

"Jaina—"

"Of course, you might not want to build a new lightsaber at first. It might be too painful. You could wait a couple of years for that. I'm sure Uncle Luke would—"

"*Jaina*," Zekk's voice was firm. "Jaina, look at me." He placed both hands on her shoulders and gave her a gentle shake.

She hadn't even realized that she'd been avoiding his gaze. Her brandy-brown eyes swung up to lock with his. Beneath his eyes the dark semicircles were like reflections of inner shadows, of hovering guilt.

"I'm not the same person I was when you knew me before, Jaina. I *can't* be. Not anymore. And you're not the same person either."

"But you're back now," Jaina objected. "We can start over." She knew the words were wrong even as she said them.

Sad. His eyes looked so sad. . . . For her?

"Maybe you can't understand where I've been . . . or *what* I've been. I'm not an innocent anymore. I've known real power and used it. I've killed face-to-face and been proud of it. That's not something I can forget."

Jaina wanted to look away, but his emerald eyes burned with a truth she couldn't escape.

"I can't erase everything and go back to

what I was," Zekk said. His voice dropped to a whisper. "Even if it were possible, I'm not sure I'd do it. I can't just pretend that nothing's changed."

Jaina wasn't sure she understood, but she nodded anyway.

"You're right about one thing, though," Zekk said. "This is a new start. For me, and for all of us. I can't go back, but I *can* go forward."

Jaina felt the threatening sting of tears and blinked them away. "What will you do?" She didn't want him to leave.

"I don't know yet, but I can't stay here. Not at the Jedi academy."

Zekk's hands gripped her shoulders so tightly that Jaina wondered if she'd have bruises. The tension between them was almost unbearable. She could sense his inner torment and his need for healing . . . for understanding.

Jaina swallowed hard. Zekk *was* different, and she had no advice or wisdom to give that could help him. He would have to find his own path. She offered the one thing she had left to give him. "Wherever you go, whatever you decide to do . . . I'll still be your friend, Zekk."

He loosened his grip on her shoulders

and smiled at her. A real smile, with real strength behind it. "I'd like that." Then a mischievous glint flashed in his eyes. "You know, it's been a long time since we went for a swim together. Of course, there aren't any fountains handy, and no glowfish in the river, but . . ."

Jaina felt a surge of happiness and relief. "Race you to the water," she said.

6

SEVERAL DAYS LATER, from where he stood, Zekk could see no more than Jaina's jumpsuited legs sticking out from beneath the navigational console in the cockpit of the *Lightning Rod*. The stained brown fabric of her comfortable uniform provided a subtle contrast to the tarnished metal plates and lubricant-smeared components scattered around the floor.

After delivering his bad news about Raynar's missing father, Han Solo had departed, heading home to Coruscant. He and Chewbacca had promised to return as soon as they could.

In the meantime, Jaina had vowed to help old Peckhum fix his battered ship, which had been severely damaged during the Second Imperium's attack. The past few days of working with old Peckhum, Jaina, Jacen, Lowie, and Tenel Ka were some of the happiest times Zekk could remember.

At first Zekk had felt guilty for taking the young Jedi trainees away from rebuilding the Great Temple—since all that horrendous damage had been his fault—but Master Skywalker himself had given his blessing to restoring the *Lightning Rod* to working condition.

"I can't think of any team more competent to repair Peckhum's ship," Luke had said to them. "Leia is sending another crew of New Republic engineers, and I have plenty of students to work on the Great Temple in the meantime. Besides, I have a sense that getting this old shuttle in flying condition will turn out to be very important in ways you can't imagine."

As the companions tinkered not only with systems damaged in the Imperial attack, but with old components that should have been replaced years before, Zekk realized that the Jedi Master was right about the importance of fixing the *Lightning Rod*—collectively and personally. He found something healing about repairing the damage he had indirectly caused, something therapeutic about laboring with his friends, who did their best to accept him, despite occasional moments of awkwardness.

While both Zekk and Peckhum were competent mechanics, Jaina was absolutely in her element. She dove into the task with gleeful enthusiasm, checking the cargo ship's hull integrity, pointing out blaster-damaged plates, running diagnostics, and issuing orders like a topnotch flight mechanic. Surprised and a bit amused, Peckhum let Jaina have free rein in directing the overall repair project of his cargo vessel. Seeing how masterful and confident she was, Zekk felt warm inside.

Now, Jaina's muffled voice drifted out from under the navigational console as she wormed her way deeper into the tiny crawlspace. "Would someone please hand me some line clamps and the signal flux meter?" She waved a grimy hand, waiting for her tools.

Lowie, whose upper body was wedged into an overhead access hatch like some huge and awkward furry stowaway, responded with an unintelligible roar. Eager to help, Zekk retrieved Jaina's instruments from the top of the cockpit panels.

With a murmured thank-you, Jaina thumped around underneath the navigation console. "There," she said at last, "that ought to do it. Now try the hyperchart function again."

Zekk flicked a few switches and pressed a button. A holographic map of several recommended hyperspace routes shimmered in front of him. "That's got it," he confirmed. "Seems to be working fine now."

Jaina scrambled out from under the console. She shook back her straight brown hair and wiped her greasy palms on the front of her rumpled flight suit, leaving dark handprints on the brown fabric. "A few finishing touches, and this ship will be ready to fly again, better than ever."

Zekk gave Jaina an uncertain smile as he offered her a hand so that she could stand up. "I can't think of anyone I'd rather have beside me fixing this ship. I bet the *Lightning Rod* hasn't been in such good shape since Peckhum first got her. Hard to believe you started with nothing more than this battered hulk and a pile of spare parts."

Jaina bit her lower lip, and her cheeks flushed pink at the compliment. "It was all of us really, working together as a team . . . including you, Zekk."

The young man nodded. He knew what she was hoping, but he couldn't stay. He *couldn't* change his mind. "I'll be leaving as soon as we're finished with the *Lightning Rod*," he said.

"I know, I know," Jaina said. "Have you decided yet where you'll go once you leave Yavin 4?"

"I've got a lot of possibilities, I guess." He shrugged. "I asked Peckhum if he'd give me a lift back to Coruscant. From there . . . who knows?"

Jaina looked away. "Whenever you finally decide what to do with your life, I hope it includes us."

Zekk wasn't sure what to say. He couldn't make any promises at this point. He could no longer be certain of who he was or what he might become. The silence stretched like a taut wire between them.

"Come on," Jaina said at last, breaking the tension and meeting his eyes, "let's go help Jacen and Tenel Ka finish patching the outer hull."

Two days later, his bags packed with a few meager possessions, Zekk stood with his old friend and companion Peckhum, saying his goodbyes to the young Jedi Knights before boarding the *Lightning Rod*.

With one hand on Zekk's shoulder, Peckhum said, "This old ship's seen some hard use, boy—of course, so have you—but you'd never know it to look at 'er now. Like a brand-new transport, with a dozen years of service left in her."

Zekk felt a warm tingle of pride at what he and his friends had accomplished. "It's like the *Lightning Rod* has a new life," he agreed.

"Yep," old Peckhum said, looking with great seriousness at the young man beside him. He cleared his throat, as if he had to force the words past some internal blockage. "That's . . . why I want you to have her. Take her for your own, Zekk—the *Lightning Rod* is my gift to you."

Jaina gasped. Lowie gave a curious rumble, and Em Teedee added, "Oh, my!"

Zekk blinked before shaking his head, not certain he'd heard right. "I couldn't. I—I . . . How would you make your living?"

"Well," Peckhum said slowly, "truth is, Chief of State Organa Solo has been after me to modernize a bit. Wants me to use some newfangled cargo ship the New Republic has. They got it for me a year or more ago, because I've been doing so much work for the Jedi academy. But you know me and new things, so I've been resisting the offer. Guess it's got some kind of improved guidance system, a code encryption whatchamacallit, and a bigger cargo hold. Gotta have more space now that there'll be more supplies to bring back and forth to Yavin 4, you know—what with all the new guardian systems and added troops stationed in orbit."

"But you've had the *Lightning Rod* ever since I've known you, Peckhum," Zekk said.

A fond smile crossed the old man's grizzled face. "Yep, I'd had 'er a few years even before you stowed away aboard her. You were a bold scamp, all right, stowin' away from ship to ship after that disaster wiped out your family and your colony on Ennth."

Zekk remembered. "They wanted me to live in their refugee stations before finding me some sort of foster home."

"Yep," Peckhum said. "And instead you found yourself a home with me."

Zekk's throat tightened. "You've done a lot for me over the years, Peckhum. I can't take your ship, too."

"To tell the truth, the *Lightning Rod*'s more of a junk heap than anything— a menace to the galaxy, really. You'd be doin' me a favor to take 'er off my hands for me. That's the only way I'll ever get around to using that new ship. We've all got to move up to bigger and better things, boy. Don't be so resistant to change."

Despite his bold words, Zekk could see that old Peckhum was choked up at the thought of parting with the *Lightning Rod*. It was as if it were a part of him. Oh, well, Zekk thought, at least this way he'd have a piece of his friend wherever he went. A piece of home.

"All right," he said. "I accept. But only if you're sure."

"I'm sure . . . I'll miss you," Peckhum said in a low voice. Then with a bit of bluster he added, "But I won't miss this old garbage scow, not for a minute." He kicked the boarding ramp. The toe of his boot clanged on the metal.

The emotion of the moment nearly overwhelmed Zekk, but he pasted a crooked smile on his face. "I can always tell when you're lying, Peckhum," he said.

Peckhum's face broke into a broad grin. "I never could fool you, boy. You and the *Lightning Rod* are two of the best friends I ever had. Take good care of each other."

Lowie woofed softly a few times. "Master

Lowbacca wishes you safe travels," Em Teedee translated.

"Live well," Tenel Ka said. "And fight only the battles worth fighting."

"We'll miss you, Zekk," Jacen said. "Don't forget to come back and visit us."

"You'll always have us as friends," Jaina said, but her voice came out in a whisper, hoarse with restrained emotion.

"I'll miss you all," Zekk said.

7

AS THE STORM system came through, a stiff breeze tore across the stubbly grass and weeds of the Great Temple's landing field. The construction scaffolding jiggled, making the balance precarious for the crew of New Republic construction workers shoring up rebuilt sections of wall.

Now that the *Lightning Rod* had departed, the young Jedi Knights turned their efforts toward fixing Lowbacca's T-23 skyhopper, which had been damaged by the Second Imperium's battle platform. While Jaina worked above, Lowie squatted beside the small craft, examining a rip in the engine compartment.

The wind suddenly gusted around the partially open cockpit, tearing free a sheet of transparisteel Jaina was attempting to fasten into the front windows. Her mind had been wandering—as usual of late, to thoughts of Zekk—when she lost her grip, and she could do nothing to grab the transparisteel in time.

Lowie howled in pain and surprise as the sheet thunked him on the head. "Oh, my," Em Teedee said. "I'm certainly glad that didn't strike *me*! My circuits could have been irreparably damaged."

Jaina leaned over the T-23's canopy, startled and abashed. "Sorry, Lowie."

The young Wookiee rubbed the bump forming beneath the dark streak of fur on his head and gave a rumble of understanding. "Master Lowbacca assures me he has sustained no permanent injury," Em Teedee said.

Jacen, who was cleaning the carbon scoring off one of the skyhopper's attitude fins, popped up, grinning. "Bet you were thinking about Zekk again—weren't you, Jaina? I can't imagine anything else that could distract you from your favorite kind of work."

Tenel Ka jumped down next to Lowie, landing with her feet spread, perfectly balanced. "I apologize. The error was mine, friend Lowbacca," she said. The warrior girl picked up the transparisteel patch and hefted it back to the top of the skyhopper.

"Jaina requested my assistance, but I was not watching when that gust struck."

"Hey, don't tell me *you* were thinking about Zekk, too," Jacen teased.

Tenel Ka shook her head emphatically; her thick red-gold braids lashed and swirled in the wind. "No, not at the moment. However, I received a message from Hapes yesterday. I am anticipating . . . something from my parents and my grandmother."

"What're you waiting for?" Jaina asked. Lowie added his own questioning growl. Jaina leaned down and tossed the lanky Wookiee a tube of metal cement.

"Hey, I'll bet she's waiting for me to tell her a joke," Jacen said. "Isn't that right, Tenel Ka?"

"This is a fact," Tenel Ka answered with a perfectly straight face. "But in addition to your joke, I have been waiting for a . . . delivery."

"What is it?" Jaina asked.

"Don't tell me," Jacen said. "Uncle Luke has asked for some rancors from Dathomir to help with the rebuilding project. That'd be great, wouldn't it? I always wanted to see one up close." Then he paused, as if considering whether he really meant it. "Well . . ."

"I believe," Tenel Ka said, nodding toward a pair of ships that had just appeared on the jungle horizon, "this is the delivery I have been expecting."

Lowie and Jaina scrambled to get a better look. A strong wind caught at the Wookiee's ginger fur, making it flutter in tufts like dozens of tiny pennants. The two ships were approaching carefully because of the unpredictable gusts and crosswinds.

Jaina studied the design of the craft approaching them. "They look vaguely Hapan, but not a design I'm familiar with."

Jacen groaned. "This isn't one of those diplomatic visits, is it? No offense, Tenel Ka, but if you're expecting one of your grandmother's associates, I think I'd prefer to clean the kitchens for a while. I hope Ambassador Yfra isn't out of prison already!"

"If this were one of my grandmother's diplomatic associates," Tenel Ka answered wryly, "perhaps I would join you at the cleaning chores. But I am expecting a gift."

Jaina had met Tenel Ka's parents, the rulers of the Hapes Cluster, when she and the other young Jedi Knights had gone there after Tenel Ka's lightsaber accident. Although Isolder and Teneniel Djo were as protective of their daughter as any parents, they had strongly supported Tenel Ka's wish to become a Jedi Knight.

"At first I refused to consider their offer of such an extravagant gift," the warrior girl went on, "but they were concerned for my safety after our battle with the Shadow Academy. In the end I agreed; only my pride had caused me to resist in the first place." She quirked an eyebrow. "My grandmother is now hoping I will reconsider accepting a prosthetic arm."

The repulsorjets of the two approaching craft set up cross breezes that sent everyone's hair flying wildly about their faces.

"I told no one about this gift except Master Skywalker," Tenel Ka said. "I had hoped to surprise you. Especially Jaina."

Jaina tried to push her wind-blown brown hair away from her face, but it was no use. "Well, okay," she said. "Surprise me."

Tenel Ka blinked her cool gray eyes. Then she raised her arm and pointed at one of the midsized Hapan ships that had just settled on the landing field.

"My parents have sent me the *Rock Dragon*. It is a ship of my own."

Jaina's mouth dropped open and she found herself at a loss for words.

"Hey, that's great, Tenel Ka," her brother said, rushing forward to look over the new ship. Lowie bellowed in delight and ran after him.

Jaina stood motionless, still thunderstruck. For years she had wanted her own ship; she had even tried to fix up the crashed TIE fighter they'd found in the jungle. On their last visit home, she had presented a list of carefully reasoned arguments to her mother. After all, if she and Jacen were old enough to fight with lightsabers, couldn't they be trusted with a small shuttle? Leia had promised to consider the idea, but preferred that the twins wait until they turned at least sixteen to have their own interstellar craft.

Her father had merely shrugged. "I know better than to argue with your mom when it comes to protecting you kids." He had flashed one of his lopsided grins and spread his arms in an expressive gesture. "Hey, if it were up to me . . ."

Each time Han came to see his children, though, he brought some sort of machinery for Jaina to work on—an old hyperdrive unit, a field flux stabilizer, a refurbished antenna dish, a mode variance inhibitor. She figured it was her father's version of a compromise—or maybe an apology.

Tenel Ka must have sensed some of Jaina's conflicting emotions. The warrior girl frowned. "You are not . . . angry? Angry that I have my own ship?" Her gray eyes looked into Jaina's. "I had hoped to ask you for a favor."

Jaina's gaze dropped, and she bit her lower lip. *Was* she angry? Lowie had his T-23, and now Tenel Ka had a ship for her personal use. But the warrior girl was one of her best friends, and she couldn't begrudge Tenel Ka this piece of good fortune. Feeling guilty over her own pettiness, Jaina shook her head. "Just a bit jealous, I guess."

"In that case, perhaps the favor is not fair to you. I had no great wish to own a ship, though for my parents' sake it was right to accept it. I had hoped that—should the need arise—Jacen and I could provide communications, weaponry, and navigational support, if you and Lowbacca would consent to serve as pilot and copilot . . . ? And chief mechanics, of course."

Jaina's head snapped back up and she gave a whoop of delight nearly as loud as the howling of the wind as the storm continued to build.

"Then you will consider my request?" Tenel Ka asked, her warrior braids rippling in the wind like velvety red-gold ribbons.

Jaina was sure her father and mother would not object to such an arrangement. After all, Jaina would simply be helping a friend now and then. She grinned broadly. "I think you've got yourself a crew."

Accompanying Tenel Ka, Jaina bounded over to where her brother and Lowie were already examining the compact vessel.

"Hey, this isn't a very new ship, Tenel Ka," Jacen said.

Tenel Ka rapped her fist against a stained spot on the hull with a satisfying thud. "This is a fact," she said.

"Lowie says the sublight engines need a tune-up," Jacen added.

"Looks like that comm transmitter's out of alignment, too," Jaina observed.

"I don't get it," Jacen said. "Your parents can afford the best that credits can buy. How come they sent you an old clunker instead of a luxury speeder?"

Jaina ran a shrewd eye over the craft. "I'm not familiar with this type of ship, but I'll bet she's got it where it counts," she said, "no matter what she looks like on the outside."

"Ah. Aha," Tenel Ka said. "My parents reasoned that it would be unwise to call attention to my personal vessel by making it elegant and luxurious." A rare smile quirked the corner of Tenel Ka's mouth. "Also, I believed Jaina and Lowbacca would prefer a ship they could spend time tinkering with."

Jaina realized that her friend was right. She chuckled. "This is a fact."

"The *Rock Dragon* has significant advantages, too," Tenel Ka went on. "For example, my grandmother helped decide which subsystems to install, adding many items no standard ship would carry. Also, it displays no markings of the Royal House of Hapes, nothing to mark it as a potential target."

"I guess that makes sense. A nondescript ship wouldn't attract attention from assassins or any other enemies," Jacen said. "Who named it the *Rock Dragon*, anyway—kind of strange, isn't it?"

"I named the ship myself. On Hapes, ships are often called 'dragon.' The term 'rock dragon' comes from Dathomir, though. It is a child's nickname for an animal I once saw there," Tenel Ka said. "Small, but highly dangerous. The creature has rough mottled skin that acts as camouflage when it hides in the rocks to guard its nest. A rock dragon eats only plants and insects, but if attacked, it defends its nest ferociously and stings its enemy. Its poison is strong enough to kill a full-grown rancor."

Jacen whistled.

"Good name for a ship," Jaina said. "Let's take it for a short spin."

8

THE CONTROLS OF the *Lightning Rod* felt good in his hands. As he left Yavin 4 behind, turning away from the Jedi academy, Zekk knew that he had his whole life ahead of him and the whole universe to choose from. . . .

But he didn't know where to go.

Peckhum had shown him how to maneuver the battered craft during their close-knit days on Coruscant, when the old man had often taken his young friend along on supply runs. Back then, with no one but each other to rely on, Zekk and Peckhum had been partners in all their grand plans.

The grizzled trader was independent, bouncing from job to job, trying to make ends meet in whatever way he could. Zekk had operated as a scavenger in the planet-wide city's lower levels, occasionally spending time with his unlikely friends Jaina and Jacen Solo.

Now, though, he had only himself . . . and he needed to choose a destination.

Zekk drifted out of the Yavin system, reveling in his freedom, the freedom to sever ties with his troubled past. He could create a new life for himself, start over and do things right this time—if only he could escape from the shadow-blot that continued to fill him, no matter how much light he tried to draw in.

After hours of aimless cruising, unwilling to dive into hyperspace without a preset course, Zekk finally selected a place to go.

He would go *home*.

But not to any of the worlds in the Core Systems, where the Shadow Academy and Lord Brakiss had made him an integral part of their struggle for a Second Imperium. No, those planets would never be *home*, no matter how much he tried to convince himself otherwise.

And not back to Coruscant either. That place held too many bad memories for him, too much past.

He wanted to go where he could forget his last few years and start anew . . . a place he could still think of as home: the planet Ennth. That was where he had come from, where he had spent the first eight years of his life, where his parents had died in the recurring disaster that struck that world every eight years.

Zekk had been born on Ennth. Less than a year later, he and his parents had moved to one of the crowded and dirty refugee stations in orbit near Ennth, as his people waited for the planetary convulsions to subside so that the colonists could return and rebuild their ruined cities on the scorched ground. Zekk had been only a child when the new settlements—ambitious structures and waterways—were erected from prefabricated modules.

The fresh ash that had rained down from erupting volcanoes made Ennth's agricultural lands fertile. Civilization on the planet had blossomed frantically during those quiet years, like a desperate flower in the desert after a rain, pouring its energy into a brief flash of life before time and the environment ultimately claimed it.

Zekk had been nine when the year of disasters returned. A bright and promising child, he had been evacuated and sent again to the crowded refugee stations, where he was expected to endure a miserable existence for many months . . . until the cycle of reconstruction and growth could begin all over.

That time, though, his parents had stayed on the surface too long, retrieving their last meaningless possessions, trying to salvage everything they had planted, as well as their furniture and mementos. A groundquake had struck unexpectedly. The seismic shock, larger than all previous ones, had its epicenter directly on New Hopetown, the village Zekk had helped build, the place a small boy had called home. Fissures opened up. Lava spewed forth. . . .

And no one had survived.

Orphaned at only nine, his home destroyed, young Zekk had been smart enough to realize that he did not want to stay without guardians on a world that proved so resistant to human settlement.

Acting brashly, Zekk had stowed away on one of the supply ships, not knowing where he was headed or where his luck would take him.

Luck. He'd always had a knack for finding things, choosing the right path. It had seemed a coincidence back then, but Brakiss had taught Zekk that he had an aptitude for using the Force. It had helped Zekk escape from Ennth.

From that point on, he had hopped from one ship to another, scrounging a life for himself. He had finally hooked up with old Peckhum, who treated him with kindness and caring, giving him a chance.

Now it was time to go home.

He scoured the *Lightning Rod*'s navicomputer records, projecting holographic paths from the generator Jaina had newly repaired, as he searched for the proper coordinates. Ennth, by no means a popular world, was located on no major trade routes.

Luckily, Peckhum had several obscure navigational files—including records of the previous evacuation. Zekk was surprised to see that the old man had been to Ennth during the initial supply runs, helping to take people off the planet. Peckhum had never told Zekk. . . . Maybe his old friend felt somewhat responsible for not staying to do more for the colonists.

Zekk punched in the coordinates, anxious to see how much the anguished world had changed since he had left it. Eight years had passed.

The *Lightning Rod* shot into hyperspace.

• • •

When the planet appeared in front of him, long-forgotten memories flashed through Zekk's mind. He sat in the pilot's chair, powering up the comm system as the *Lightning Rod* settled into normal space again and approached Ennth.

The large moon had a pocked and cratered appearance, as if it held many mouths full of fangs waiting to devour human settlements on the primary world. The moon's path was highly elliptical, oscillating around Ennth in an endless planetary dance. Once every eight years the orbit brought the two celestial partners so close together that the moon grazed Ennth's atmosphere. Tidal forces and increased gravity cracked the ground, sparked volcanic eruptions, and kneaded the world's surface, producing groundquakes and tidal waves. Hurricanes and storms destroyed anything on the exposed ground, while the approaching moon ripped away portions of the atmosphere, which was replenished by the volcanic outgassing from Ennth's interior.

Now Zekk saw a bustling flotilla in orbit: merchant ships, rescue ships, traders, and a motley assortment of ragtag vessels, as well as huge cargo haulers that had been stripped of their hyperdrive engines to make more room for living quarters inside.

Refugee stations. Zekk recognized them from his previous unpleasant time spent aboard.

He had come at just the right moment, when people and his homeworld needed him the most. The colonists were evacuating Ennth again. This could be a way for him to redeem himself, a time to focus only on helping others.

The giant moon hovered close in the sky, hurtling along in its disruptive orbit. Zekk shuddered as a half-forgotten fear leaped within him. But he drove it back. He would have to rise above his fears if he was going to make a difference here.

The disaster was about to strike again.

9

JACEN RUSHED INTO the communication center and looked around at the mind-boggling display of equipment the New Republic engineers were installing. He couldn't see any cause for an emergency, but Raynar had told him he was urgently needed here.

The young blond-haired boy from Alderaan had run with him through the corridors of the Great Temple into the middle of this hotbed of repair work. The two stood panting, surrounded by all the activity.

At one station Lowie was busy rewiring the new shield generator console. Tenel Ka assembled components for a larger, sharper comm screen, holding each piece in place with her chin or a knee and then fastening it down with clamps and anchors. His sister Jaina bounced around the room with feverish enthusiasm, in the midst of twelve different projects at once.

Jacen found the excitement vaguely bewildering—it was only a bunch of components and electronics, after all . . . nothing interesting. Oh, he was competent enough at running equipment, but he didn't have an *understanding* with machines like Jaina did. Instead, Jacen had an understanding with living creatures of all sizes. He'd been in his quarters feeding his pets when Raynar had summoned him.

Now that Jacen had arrived, though, no one seemed to notice. "Hey, don't everybody greet me at once," he said. He turned to Raynar beside him. "So what's the cause for alarm?"

The blond boy adjusted his newly washed robes and tightened his sash—a dull brown sash, Jacen noticed, not a color Raynar usually wore. He wondered if it had anything to do with the disappearance of his father.

"They, uh, said some creature got into a transformer housing," he stammered, darting nervous glances toward the back of the room. "Tenel Ka suggested you might be able to coax it out, so I, um, ran to get you."

It gave Jacen a warm feeling to know Tenel Ka had thought of him to solve a problem. Even with only one arm, she had proved herself so good at everything she did that Jacen often felt like a bumbling buffoon around her. But Tenel Ka had *asked* for him—and this was something he was good at. He would be proud to help her.

He grinned at Raynar, but the other boy didn't grin back.

"Do you think it's safe?" Raynar asked hesitantly. "The creature might be poisonous."

Jacen shut his eyes for a moment and sent a thought searching through the room, past the flurry of Jedi students and New Republic engineers. . . .

There. He had it. Jacen opened his eyes. "Well, it's not a crystal snake, if that's what you're worried about. Nothing dangerous."

"Well, if you're sure, I'll go back to my station," Raynar said, twisting his brown sash into knots around his fingers.

"This'll take just a few minutes," Jacen answered. "There's nothing lurking anywhere near your comm console. Don't worry." Raynar nodded and cautiously went back to his workstation.

Jacen headed to where Tenel Ka worked quickly and methodically, clad only in her lizard-hide armor, a pair of boots, and a tool belt. "Hey, Tenel Ka. How do you tell the difference between a rancor?" he asked brightly.

Tenel Ka turned her cool gray eyes toward him and raised an eyebrow. "I believe that one of its legs are both the same."

Jacen blinked in surprise. "You've heard that one before?"

"Yes." Tenel Ka did not stop working. "Please hold this. Thank you. Your joke is a well-known piece of non-sequitur humor from my mother's clan on Dathomir. Most people don't understand it—even fewer find it funny."

Jacen slapped his forehead. "I should have known. Anyway, Raynar said you wanted to see me."

"Ah. Aha." She gestured toward a metallic box fastened near the ceiling. "I had hoped you could convince the creature to leave the power transformer housing before it comes to harm, or before it causes any damage to the circuitry."

"Hey, that's great, Tenel Ka. I think you're really starting to understand how I feel about animals and why I like to collect pets."

"Perhaps," she said. Then in a drier voice she added, "I also had no wish to *dis*assemble and *re*assemble the transformer housing."

Jacen felt himself flush. Well, at least

she had asked for his help, which was rare enough for Tenel Ka.

Jacen rolled a portable piece of lightweight scaffolding against the wall, locked it into place, then clambered up to where the uninvited reptilian guest had hidden. Placing his palm under a hole in the transformer housing, Jacen sent enticing thoughts to the creature inside. *Warm. Safe. Warm. Food.*

He concentrated, adding reassurance and calm thoughts, tempting the creature. In less than a minute, a spotted thyrsl slithered out and curled happily on Jacen's palm. Long and flexible, the thyrsl looked like a skinny snake with twelve tiny legs.

"You just crawled in there for the heat, didn't you?" Jacen crooned, cupping it in his hand. "Don't worry, I'll take you someplace that's nice and warm." He turned, holding on to the scaffolding with his free hand, careful to maintain his balance. Out of the corner of his eye, Jacen caught a flash of brightly colored robes.

"I just got a message that a ship's coming down to the landing clearing, on final approach," Raynar said. "It's the *Millennium Falcon* returning from Coruscant."

Jacen was just clambering down to the next level of the scaffolding. "Hey, Dad didn't tell us he was coming back again so soon—" He loosened his hold for only a moment, but his balance was off. Trying to protect the thyrsl from harm, he tumbled backward toward the floor—

—only to be caught on a cushion of air just centimeters before he hit the flagstones. Jacen touched down lightly and breathed a sigh of relief. He raised his head to see Tenel Ka and Raynar standing together, locked in concentration.

Concern was written all over the Alderaan boy's flushed face. He swirled the sleeves of his colored robes. "Sorry I distracted you, Jacen. Are you all right?"

Tenel Ka stretched out her arm and helped Jacen to his feet. "It takes a good deal of practice," she said, "to climb with only one hand."

"No kidding," Jacen said. He held up his other hand to show her the thyrsl. "At least we're both safe and sound," he added, a bit sheepishly. Once again, he had bumbled in front of Tenel Ka! There didn't seem to be any easy way to impress her.

Jaina and Lowie had rushed over in response to Raynar's announcement. After seeing that her brother was all right despite the mishap, Jaina grinned mischievously at him. "Nice maneuver, laser brain."

Lowie gave an urf of laughter.

To cover his embarrassment, Jacen turned to Raynar. "Hey, let's go meet Dad and see if he's heard anything about your father."

The other boy perked up, showing sudden, intense interest.

Jacen cradled the thyrsl as they all ran out of the communications center. Along the way, he would find a warm spot on some sunbaked stones, well away from the reconstruction work, where the creature couldn't cause any more mischief.

10

YAVIN'S SUN WAS bright and the jungle air warm, with a light breeze but none of the strong winds they had experienced a few days earlier. When Han Solo and Chewbacca strode out of the *Falcon*, Jaina turned to look behind her. Raynar stood alone a small distance away, twisting his brown sash around his fingers, his eyes averted from the happy family reunion.

Han noticed him, too. He flashed a quick grin at Jaina and Jacen. His eyes, though, were serious. "Got a surprise for you kids from home, but let me talk to Raynar first."

The young Alderaan boy looked up hopefully. Jaina saw her father shake his head. "No news, actually," Han Solo admitted. "But we've got some solid leads. If your father made it somewhere safe, we're hoping he'll try to get a message to you. In the meantime, we've got Lando Calrissian and some of the best ex-smugglers in the New Republic on the search."

"I understand," Raynar said, then turned and walked dejectedly back toward the Great Temple, his bright robes drooping around him.

With forced good humor after the sad news for Raynar, Han rubbed his hands together. "Ready for your surprise?" Han turned to yell up the ramp. "C'mon out."

"Anakin!" Jaina exclaimed as their brother appeared in the opening.

"Hey, what're you doing here?" Jacen asked, giving his little brother a playful punch on the shoulder.

"It's a long story," Anakin said, sweeping his straight dark bangs away from his ice-blue eyes. "You see, I had an idea for restoring the Great Temple. You know how much I like to take things apart and put them together again. I've always been good at puzzles."

"Well, this one has an awful lot of pieces," Jaina said, looking doubtfully at the piles of broken stones lying about. She dismissed a flickering thought that the whole place felt much bleaker, much emptier, since Zekk had departed.

"I suggested that we could treat the

temple like a puzzle—sort out the pieces, then fit them back together again. I figured I could see the patterns in my mind," Anakin continued. "Any areas that we can't reconstruct from the original stones can be reproduced by New Republic artists so they'll look just like the original Massassi work." He held up a little hologram of the Great Temple, taken long ago when it had been used as a hidden Rebel base. "We'll use this as a template."

"Well, at least I have *one* brother who's a genius," Jaina said, tossing Jacen a teasing look.

"Mom seemed so excited by the idea that I sort of volunteered to come to Yavin 4, even though it's not time for my classes to start again," Anakin went on. "I'm not sure how it happened. I just said that I'd be one of the best people for putting together the puzzle pieces, and Dad said he'd help, and Mom seemed so happy. . . ." He spread his hands, looking a bit confused. "And here I am."

Han put a comforting hand on his younger son's shoulder. "Don't worry, kid. Your mom just has that effect on people. That's how she got Chewie and me to help with her crazy Rebellion against the Empire." The older Wookiee groaned at the memory.

"Yeah," Jaina said, pondering, "and I remember that time Lowie and I volunteered to map out the orbits of space debris over Coruscant."

Jacen added, "And then you and Lowie offered to help fix old Peckhum's space station, too." This time, Lowie groaned.

"Getting people to volunteer is one of your mother's many gifts," Han concluded. "That's why she's a politician."

Anakin looked over to where Luke Skywalker and some of his students were still collecting chunks of rock that had been blasted from the top of the temple pyramid. "Well, little brother," Jaina said, "what are you waiting for?"

Anakin took a deep breath and blew it out. "I volunteered—I guess I'd better get started." He trotted off toward the Great Temple.

"I brought you each a little gift, as usual," Han said, producing a smooth, pearl-pink sphere and offering it to Jacen. "It's a gort egg."

"Wow, I've always wanted one of these," Jacen said. "They make great pets—kind of like miniature woolamanders with really soft feathers. You can even teach them to talk."

"It'll take almost a year to hatch," Han warned, "and you have to keep it warm the whole time."

"No problem," Jacen assured him, looking over at his sister. "Uh—is it, Jaina?"

She pretended to heave a deep sigh. "I think I can manage to build you a temperature-controlled cage, Jacen."

"And for you, Jaina . . ." Han held out a meter-long chain of devices that looked like a rope of Corellian nerf sausages. "A modular signal transmitter."

"Great! More components for my collection," Jaina said, grinning.

"Don't thank me too soon," Han said. "The transmitter works, but this is such an old model that it doesn't have much range."

"That's okay, Dad—it's modular. I can figure out a way to link in a higher-powered signal booster," Jaina said, feeling her spirits lift at the prospect of this new mechanical challenge.

Jacen asked, as if the thought had suddenly struck him, "Why is it so important to Mom to rebuild the Great Temple just like it was? I mean, the Massassi weren't a particularly honorable race. Is she just doing this for Uncle Luke?"

"No," Han said. "There's more to it than that. You kids never really saw the planet Alderaan, where your mom grew up, since it was destroyed before you were born."

"We've seen holoclips," Jaina pointed out. "And those framed images you gave her."

Han nodded absently. "Alderaan was a center of culture and education. Peaceful planet . . . lots of artists, philosophers, musicians. Grand Moff Tarkin made your mother watch while he used the Death Star to blast her home planet into tiny little chunks. Ever since then, anything the Empire ruined, your mom's tried to set right again. And in her memory, Yavin 4 was our first safe haven after your uncle Luke and I rescued her from the Death Star. For her, the Great Temple is a symbol of the Rebellion's struggle to build a fair government for everyone in the galaxy. So it's kind of a personal thing. Mom'll be coming here in six or seven days to check on our progress."

"Hey, she'll be here for her birthday then," Jacen said, counting the days.

"We thought it would be nice to have the whole family together for a change," Han said. "Even if we have to come here to do it."

"Dad," Jaina said. "Jacen and I have been trying to come up with just the perfect gift for Mom's birthday. We thought that maybe if we went to the Alderaan system and got a special piece of Mom's planet, one that she could take with her wherever she went, like a keepsake. . . ."

"Yeah," Han said in a soft voice, raising his eyebrows in surprise. "Yeah, I think your mom'd like that. But I don't have time to take you kids there. I've got to help with the work here, not to mention keeping up with the search for Raynar's father."

"Well, we could go by ourselves in Tenel Ka's ship," Jaina said, trying to hide her expression of eagerness and fervent hope.

Han looked even more surprised. "Oh, yeah. I forgot about the *Rock Dragon*. Tenel Ka's parents contacted Leia for permission to station a Hapan ship here."

"You mean we can go then?" Jaina said.

"I didn't say that. . . ." Han frowned, as if thinking it over seriously. "Well, all right," he said at last. "But only on two conditions."

"Anything," Jaina said, and her brother nodded.

"First, you have to let Chewie and me check out the ship personally, so we know it's safe for you to fly. Second, I want you back here in three days. No more. Just to Alderaan and back—no sightseeing, no joyriding."

"We promise," Jaina said. "What could possibly go wrong?"

In the end, Han and Chewie found nothing more significant than a rear stabilizer to replace on the *Rock Dragon*. By the next morning, the ship was ready for its flight to the Alderaan system.

"Not a bad little hunk of machinery," Han said to Tenel Ka, looking around the cockpit approvingly. "Did they set it up specially so you could fly it with one hand?"

"The controls have been adjusted to make that possible," Tenel Ka said. "But Jaina has agreed to act as pilot."

Han crossed his arms over his vest, wearing a look of fatherly pride. "A Solo at the helm, huh? Good choice."

Jaina sighed in relief at her father's response. "And Lowie's going to be my copilot," she said. Chewbacca pounded a hairy fist on his nephew's shoulder.

"I'm all ready," Jacen said. He tossed his

duffel into a storage net, plopped down in one of the passenger's seats, and buckled his crash webbing.

"I am also prepared," Tenel Ka said, seating herself beside Jacen. "Jaina, you may depart when ready."

Lowie took the copilot's seat with an enthusiastic bellow, and Jaina strapped herself in at the pilot's station.

"Three days now," Han Solo called after them. "I have your word on it."

Jaina looked at her father and rolled her eyes. "We'll be fine, Dad. We're just going to get a piece of rock. If we're not back in three days, you have my personal permission to send out a search party."

"Hey, if I can't trust my own kids, who can I trust?" Han shrugged, a lopsided smile glued to his face, but Jaina could tell her father was struggling to look nonchalant. Then he and Chewie left the ship and stood outside on the landing field.

As the *Rock Dragon* took off, Jaina risked a glance away from her piloting tasks to watch her father and Chewie waving goodbye. Something felt strange, she thought.

Maybe she just wasn't used to being on *this* side of the cockpit viewports, looking out at her father.

11

WHEN THE *ROCK Dragon* reached the graveyard of Alderaan, Jaina stared out the front windowport, sensing the forever-magnified instant of despair that had accompanied the destruction of an entire planet.

Only this jagged, broken rubble remained of her mother's homeworld. Princess Leia had grown up here, living in a sparkling white city on an island in the middle of a crater lake, soaring in giant repulsor-freighters across the peaceful grasslands, resting in solitude in the ancient organic structures built by a long-extinct insect race. . . .

Sitting in the pilot's seat of the Hapan passenger cruiser, Jaina surveyed the countless flying splinters of rock scattered in space before her: huge boulders, small pebbles, congealed lumps of pitted metal.

Each piece of debris was like a tombstone for the dead of Alderaan.

In the copilot's chair, Lowie chuffed and growled, pointing at the dangerous swarms of rocks. Their navigation console displayed a thickly interwoven web of projected orbital paths.

With her rudimentary understanding of his Wookiee dialect, Jaina was able to decipher some of the words Lowie spoke, but Em Teedee translated anyway. "Master Lowbacca feels this asteroid field will be most challenging to his navigational and piloting abilities. Personally, I feel it my duty to point out the potential hazards, should you choose to proceed. Asteroid fields can be extremely dangerous."

Jaina pressed her lips together, her expression grim. "This isn't just any asteroid field, Em Teedee—this isn't natural. This used to be a planet, but it was blown to bits by the Death Star. It was my mother's planet."

The other young Jedi Knights fell silent, feeling the intangible grief that surrounded the place, mourning those peaceful millions who had died here because of the Empire's brutality.

Jaina stared at the crumbling shards,

knowing that the bones of Alderaan's population drifted out there somewhere, as well, now little more than cosmic dust. All the great buildings and cities: the revered Alderaan University; Crevasse City, built right into canyon walls; Terrarium City, famed as a metropolis under glass. . . .

Jaina had seen images of Alderaan in its glory. Her mother kept a gallery of paintings that showed her beloved homeworld. Han Solo had given them to Leia around the time of their wedding.

She had heard her mother tell the story many times of how she had been a prisoner aboard the Death Star, forced to watch as Grand Moff Tarkin used the deadly battle station to obliterate the peaceful planet. Tarkin had given no warning, allowed none of the population to escape.

Now only this rubble field remained.

As far as she knew, Leia had never returned to the Alderaan system. Jaina guessed that the sight would always be too painful, but hoped that a special shard of her mother's destroyed home would make a fine memento.

She gripped the controls of the *Rock Dragon*. "You ready, Lowie?" she said. "We're going inside."

"Oh, do be careful," Em Teedee said.

Jacen and Tenel Ka quietly checked their crash webbing, but did not interrupt the two pilots as they cruised into the scattershot storm of planetary debris. Around them, the rocks coursed and ricocheted, spinning about to display jagged edges, raw craters. Over two decades, the debris had collided again and again, slowly settling into an organized cloud. Some of the shards clung together through their own gravity, gradually fusing into clusters of rock.

"This place has a strong . . . feel to it," Tenel Ka said. "As if I sense the ghosts of . . . many life forces obliterated at once."

Jacen nodded. "Uncle Luke talks about how there was a great disturbance in the Force when Alderaan was destroyed."

"I still feel a disturbance," Tenel Ka said. "Like echoes."

Jaina scanned the debris with the ship's sensors. Some of the meteoroids were composed of rock, others of metals from different portions of the planet—the crust, the mantle, the core.

Lowie barked a comment, and Em Teedee translated. "Master Lowbacca wishes to know what, exactly, he should be searching for."

"Something . . . special," Jaina answered.

Jacen added, "But we don't know what it is yet."

The asteroids grew denser around them. Lowie flicked his yellow gaze down to the labyrinth of orbital paths diagrammed on the screen. Jaina saw the lines tightening up, the paths becoming more congested.

"Time for some fancy flying, Lowie," she said, then smiled back over her shoulder at Tenel Ka. "Let's see what the *Rock Dragon* has to show for itself."

"Oh, my," Em Teedee said.

The Hapan passenger cruiser skimmed between two of the larger asteroids and circled back, curving below the plane of the debris cluster and then arrowing back through again. While simultaneously flying, watching out for obstacles, and studying the navigational diagram, Jaina continued to glance at the sensors, searching for exactly the right place to go. She felt she would know the place by instinct, as soon as she laid eyes upon it.

When she let her attention flicker for just a moment, Lowie bellowed in surprise and wrenched the copilot controls, spinning the *Rock Dragon* in a backward loop to avoid a jagged splinter of stone. He arced back in a U-turn and returned the way they had come. Their ship plunged once more through the rubble field.

"Hey, Jaina, are you sure you know where you're going?" Jacen said.

Lowie growled something reassuring, then performed another U-turn to head back through the rocks.

"This is kind of fun," Jaina said, accelerating as she circled around one of the larger chunks so that they could see the cratered landscape below them.

"I am glad you approve of our Hapan technology, Captain," Tenel Ka said. "My grandmother assured me you would approve of the special modifications she ordered to this ship."

"I'm not sure I understand all the features of the engines and their subsystems yet," Jaina answered, "but that leaves more for me to tinker with. A pilot's duty, you know. Thanks for giving me the chance to fly this, Tenel Ka."

Jacen kept peering out the side window, shaking his head. "It's amazing to think this was once a whole planet. . . . Alderaan. I heard that some smugglers or pirates had been using this rubble as a relay station or a hideout, just like the asteroid field around Hoth."

Tenel Ka grunted. "There will always be such stories. Some are true, others are not. I doubt we will find pirates here."

Jaina let Lowie handle the flying while she studied the sensors again, hoping to spot that special *something* she was looking for. The Hapan ship had plenty of unusual diagnostic devices; it seemed as if Tenel Ka's grandmother had installed every imaginable system. But Jaina used only the diagnostics with which she was most familiar, analyzing rocks, looking for something out of the ordinary.

A special gift for her mother.

When the bizarre asteroid showed up on her screens, Jaina knew instantly that she had found their target.

"Lowie, here's our new course," she said, highlighting one of the blips among the green lines on the navigational projection panel.

The large asteroid reflected light from the Alderaan system's distant sun. Its surface was pockmarked and pitted, but it gleamed with a metallic sheen. The readings indicated that this asteroid was almost pure metal, with a higher concentration of precious elements than any other in the asteroid field.

They had discovered a lump from the true core of Alderaan, the heart of her mother's world. The other young Jedi Knights leaned forward to see as the *Rock Dragon* approached the asteroid.

"That's the one," Jaina said.

12

AS HE SCANNED the surface of Ennth, Zekk was surprised to find scattered settlements in the same locations where previous cities had been destroyed eight years before.

Zekk adjusted the *Lightning Rod*'s course and guided it into the stream of shuttle traffic toward the main settlement, where his parents had lived, where they had made their dreams. . . . He remembered that the colonists optimistically renamed the villages each time— New Hopetown, Newer Hopetown, and Newest Hopetown. He wondered what they would do once they ran out of qualifiers.

Powering up the ship's comm system, Zekk transmitted a message to the central control barracks, identifying himself. He briefly told his story, that he was a prodigal son from Ennth who had now returned.

The communications controller greeted

him with surprise, but her voice held the breathless urgency of someone burdened with too many responsibilities. She put on another man, an operations commander named Rastur, who was in charge of the evacuation activities. Zekk thought he remembered the man: during the previous disaster, a brave young soldier named Rastur had been decorated for his heroic feats. He had apparently risen in importance and now had the primary responsibility for preserving the persistent colonists of Ennth.

As he brought the *Lightning Rod* down into the belt of stormclouds, Zekk hoped the ship wouldn't prove to be aptly named. He passed through knotted black thunderheads, roiling weather systems churned up by the oncoming moon's tidal chaos.

Below, the landscape of Ennth lay black and jumbled. Hardened lava rock stood out in cracked scabs. The broken outcroppings looked fresh and solid, laid down in the eruptions of only eight years ago.

Zekk saw green patches in the hardened rocky landscape, small jewels of farmland fertilized and tilled. To his astonishment, workers still frantically combed the fields to finish one last harvest before they had to depart from their doomed world. Those food supplies would have to last the people on the refugee stations until the Ennth colonists could reestablish their settlements on a pristine landscape in another year.

Fighting against the turbulent wind, Zekk's ship approached the remains of a bustling spaceport, a stripped-down landing area surrounded by dismantled buildings and partially torn down warehouses.

Zekk brought the *Lightning Rod* in as several cargo ships, heavily loaded with people and supplies, lumbered into the air. Barely aerodynamic, the ships wobbled as they gained altitude. Other ships came in and circled, scouting for any available landing space.

He secured the ship, opened the hatch, then bounded down the ramp, ready to help. Troops and rescue workers scurried about—volunteers, colonists, everyone doing their part. The air, smelling of smoke and sulfur, was heavy with humidity and ozone from the stormclouds overhead.

In the city square Zekk saw huge statues, colorful paintings along the sides of lava-brick walls, vibrant artistic expressions everywhere he turned—all being left behind. Each masterwork of sculpture and illustration had been carved or painted in the past eight years as an expression of thanksgiving by the colonists when they had rebuilt their demolished town.

As he stood outside the *Lightning Rod*, a young woman rushed over to meet him. She was trim, in her early twenties, wearing a comfortable utility suit, her hair dark brown and cropped close to her head. Her eyes, a deep sepia, squinted with weariness and strain.

"Are you Zekk?" she said, gesturing for him to accompany her back to the headquarters building. She began walking immediately without waiting for Zekk, as if she had no time at all for light conversation. She called over her shoulder. "Welcome to Another Hopetown. I'm Shinnan. I remember your parents from when I was thirteen years old, during the last evacuation. You were just a boy then . . . seven?"

"Almost nine," Zekk corrected. "I think I remember you, too. You were kind of a bossy girl telling the other kids what to do."

She smiled. "Yes, and now I'm a bossy woman telling grown-ups what to do. I hope you've come here to help. We could

certainly use an extra hand during the last
stages of the evacuation."

Zekk looked up into the darkening clouds.
He saw crisscrossed lines of ship exhausts
like white spiderwebs highlighted by flashes
of lightning. "I came home," he said. "I've
done a lot of things in my life, but now I've
returned to Ennth. I'll gladly lend a hand."

He hurried to keep up with Shinnan's
rapid steps. Around him he saw the foun-
dations of sheared-off buildings and tent-
covered supply stacks lashed down and
waiting to be picked up by cargo ships. The
Ennth colonists continued to work steadily
without rest, managing to look frenzied
and organized at the same time.

On the way to the main command center,
they passed abandoned buildings; some of
the roofs had collapsed, windows broken.
Tremors and aftershocks had slammed
through Ennth for the past year or so, yet
the colonists had waited until the last
minute to pack up. Partly through the
Force and partly through his own nerve
endings, Zekk felt the ground trembling
beneath his feet, as if he stood on a bomb
just waiting to explode.

The only structures still inhabited seemed

to be small stone dwellings near the command center—probably the quarters for Shinnan and Rastur and the other evacuation workers who had vowed to stay until the bitter end . . . just as his own parents had tragically done, eight years before.

The ground suddenly shook, as if a squirming krayt dragon lay just under the surface. Zekk stumbled, but Shinnan did not even pause in her step. The tremors ceased in only a few seconds. Shinnan made no comment at all as she took him inside the command center.

A lean, hard-looking man stepped up to them. His eyes were old beyond his years, with stress lines etched into his face. He carried a deep sorrow within him. "Rastur, this is Zekk—returned to us after these many years." Shinnan paused, seeing the dead look on Rastur's face. "What's wrong, my love?" She slid her arms beneath his and held him tightly.

"I received word from our reconnaissance flyers," Rastur said. "Newest Coast Town has just been destroyed."

Shinnan gasped, then composed herself. "What happened?"

"A tidal wave," he said, "undersea seismic activities. We saw it coming, but had only a few minutes' warning. The wave came in a thousand meters high and wiped out the entire settlement." He drew in a deep breath and crossed his arms over his chest. "Luckily, we had already stepped up evacuation and salvage procedures. We got eighty percent of the supplies to safety in orbit. Most of the settlers had taken refuge, except for a hundred or so who remained behind for a last run. We also lost two supply ships."

Zekk listened with growing horror, but didn't say anything. Shinnan spoke up. "Any chance for rescue operations?"

"There were no survivors," Rastur said firmly, "not even any flotsam and jetsam to salvage. . . ." His voice hitched before he brought it back under control. "In fact, there's not even much of a *coast* left where the wave hit."

Shinnan hugged the man briefly. "We knew to expect casualties, Rastur," she said. "We'll have a year to mourn once we're all off planet and waiting for the land to settle down again. For now, we've got work to do."

Finally Rastur became aware of Zekk, his eyes lighting up with a glimmer of welcome. "We're glad you've come home, Zekk—now, more than ever, we could use your help. Your people need you."

For the next few days, Zekk worked harder than he ever had in his life, filling the *Lightning Rod*'s cargo holds to capacity and flying up to the refugee stations in orbit. He got to know some of the supply runners as well as several of the colonists. Many claimed to remember him as a child; others didn't, but welcomed him anyway.

Despite the impending disaster and devastation, everyone on Ennth seemed willing to pull together as a team for a common goal, salvaging what they could from their homes and their lives, fleeing to safety before the groundquakes and volcanoes and tidal waves destroyed everything.

Many people died in the rush, some through carelessness, others through accidents. A few older colonists even dropped from sheer exhaustion, left behind to be buried by the violent upheaval of their adopted world.

In the frantic command center, Rastur never seemed to sleep, directing hundreds of shuttle flights, deciding which shipments had to go first, which colonists would be stationed on which refugee station. Shinnan did her best to assist him, taking care of the people, listening to complaints and suggestions . . . somehow managing to hold it all together.

One day later that week, lightning struck across the landscape like turbolaser bolts, blasting sand and lava rock. The winds picked up, making it difficult for the last cargo ships to take off safely. With his long dark hair tied in a ponytail to keep it out of the way, Zekk remained behind to dismantle the remaining computers from the command center, haphazardly packing them into the last few battered crates, then hauling all nonessential components away.

Rastur turned from his central post, his expression even grimmer than his usual perpetual frown. "We've just lost Heartland Settlement to lava," he said. "A chain of volcanoes ripped it to pieces and incinerated the remaining structures. Luckily the last flights had already taken off. No casualties. Minimal loss of equipment."

The other workers in the command center set up a ragged cheer. "We're all finished here at Another Hopetown, Rastur," Shinnan said. "All that remains is to pack up our own quarters and possessions."

"All right, I'm glad we left that until last. Everything else is taken care of, so I'll be able to sleep better at night," he said, "once we get off the surface and up to the refugee stations."

Shinnan stepped to the doorway of the command center. Zekk followed her, ready to offer his help, though his arms and legs felt ready to drop off. Utterly exhausted, he still felt exhilarated by how much they had accomplished despite seemingly impossible odds. Though they had suffered casualties, Ennth had been successfully evacuated.

Then the groundquake struck.

Not just a tremor like those he had experienced hundreds of times in the last few days—the seismic shock felt as if a Super Star Destroyer had crashed down on the planet, slamming into the world's crust like a giant mallet. The remaining computer stands inside the command center fell over. Other buildings surrounding the near-deserted square swayed and rocked. One of the tall statues toppled and smashed on the cobblestones.

While Zekk held the door frame and fought for balance, Shinnan sprinted across the open square. Bobbing and weaving, she headed directly toward the low stone structures that had served as living quarters for the evacuation personnel.

"Shinnan, no!" Zekk cried. He whirled to look at Rastur. "Where is she going?"

"To our home—to rescue some things she needs."

Zekk raced after her, feeling a powerful dread grow within him. He wondered if it was just his imagination . . . or an echo of premonition through the Force. He had been avoiding using his Jedi powers since the Shadow Academy's defeat, afraid he would be too tempted to make use of the dark side again.

But now he definitely sensed the athletic dark-haired woman was in grave danger. As she dashed inside the shaking building, Zekk ran toward her, but his legs wobbled and jerked as the ground bounced beneath him like a vibrodrum.

Rastur stood at the command center door, his face as ash-gray as the volcanic dust that filled the skies. His drawn lips mouthed one word as he watched Shinnan disappear inside the stone house. "No."

With a great seismic heave, the ground split in front of Zekk like a torn sheet of paper. He toppled to the cobblestones as the fissure widened, trembled, then stopped.

Zekk looked up, getting himself to his hands and knees, ready to jump across the meter-wide crack that hung open like a yawning, jagged mouth.

Then another shock struck through the ground. This time, the stone buildings did not survive—*none* of the remaining warehouses. And not the place Shinnan and Rastur had called home. The heavy roof collapsed, the walls buckled outward, and the entire structure fell in upon itself . . . crushing the young woman inside.

As the tremors subsided, Zekk finally got back to his feet. He jumped across the broken fissure and staggered to the ruins of the building. "Shinnan!" he called out.

He reached the rubble and tried to pull stone blocks away. Within moments Rastur and the remaining workers appeared at his side, instinctively knowing what to do, digging through the rubble. Rastur moved mechanically, in a daze, as if he had turned off all of his emotions. He had lost too much already to feel any greater despair.

Zekk strove with his mind, trying to find some trace of Shinnan. "Are you there? Can you hear me?" But only a cold, disturbing silence came back at him. . . .

When they found Shinnan's body half an

hour later, Zekk slumped in grief, but Rastur just stood, unmoving. In the young woman's hands she cradled an electronic datapad and a sheaf of paper.

"What were they?" Zekk said, picking them up, looking at drawings and hand-written notes. Somehow, she had considered these items important enough to die for.

"They were our plans," Rastur said, "our architectural designs for the new house we intended to build, once we moved back down to the surface . . . during resettlement."

His words were choked off, and then he spoke in a flat voice as if repeating a memorized litany. "We anticipated casualties. We always knew people would die." He whispered again, "We anticipated casualties."

Then he straightened, smartly gesturing to the other workers. "We're done here on Ennth. Load up the last ships."

Rastur looked up at the sky. "It's time to leave this place to its own destruction."

13

NUDGING THE *ROCK Dragon*'s controls, Jaina and Lowie worked together to land the Hapan passenger cruiser on what had once been the core of Alderaan. Em Teedee added his tinny voice of encouragement. "Steady, steady . . . oh, very well done, indeed!"

Jacen glanced out the windowport, his fingers pressed against the transparisteel. "Looks like you picked the right one, Jaina."

The surface of the asteroid had a rippled appearance, pitted from the rigors of space and dusty from the powdery debris that flew like a storm through the rubble field. Craters had been gouged out by smaller rocks that had slammed like orbiting bullets into the asteroid.

The *Rock Dragon* shuddered as its landing pads settled onto the surface. "We're secure," Jaina said. Lowie rumbled his agreement.

"Time to get into our gear," Jacen said. He rushed back to the storage compartment to prepare for their outside expedition, slid open the sealed door, and inspected the environment suits dangling there. "Never seen this design before. Tenel Ka, are you sure these suits are going to work for us?"

"My grandmother packed them herself," Tenel Ka answered. "She would naturally be most concerned for our safety."

"Yeah, that's a fact," Jacen said with a faint grin, thinking of the hard old woman and her unbridled ambitions.

The Hapan environment suits were sturdy but flexible, a tightly woven and completely sealed fabric that would protect them from the vacuum of space while allowing them freedom of movement. The helmets that locked to the collars reminded Jacen of exotic seashells, curved and swirled to accommodate air tubes, outside spotlights, and coolant piping. Jacen slid one helmet over his head and turned, looking through the round faceplate at the red-haired warrior girl. "How do I look?" he said.

"Would you prefer an honest answer?" Tenel Ka replied.

"It was just a rhetorical question," he mumbled, handing one of the suits to Tenel

Ka as he climbed into another. "It looks like your grandmother even remembered an extralarge one for Lowbacca."

"My grandmother paid careful attention to all such details before she allowed my parents to send me this ship," Tenel Ka said.

The companions checked each other's fastenings to verify that the suits were secure. Jacen stood back to look at his friends in their seashell-shaped helmets, head lamps, and silvery suits; they appeared sinister and ominous.

"We look like a crew of alien invaders," he said. "Like those legendary pirates of the asteroid belt, Tenel Ka."

Jaina picked up her sample packs and cutting tools and went to the magnetic hatch of the *Rock Dragon*. "What are we waiting for?" she said. "Let's go."

Stepping out onto the surface of the asteroid, Jacen felt light as a feather, ready to fly. The ships on which he had traveled had been equipped with artificial-gravity generators, but the pull from this metallic mountain in space was insufficient to hold them with more than a frail grasp.

The surface beneath his booted feet was like hardened slag. He used his boot heel to scrape away the tarnish and space dust, exposing bare metal that shone in the faint starlight. Tilting his helmet upward, he saw the other rocks overhead, boulders like clouds casting random shadows across the core asteroid.

Tenel Ka strode beside Lowie, who stood tall and hulking in his environment suit. Tenel Ka's grandmother had ordered a specially tailored suit for the young warrior girl, sealing off the extra sleeve for her missing arm so that the empty fabric would not get in her way.

Jaina trudged forward, toolkit in hand, pointing her facemask downward as she studied the pocked metal surface. She stepped to a fissure in the rock and squatted to let the light in her helmet shine into the fissure like a beacon.

"Look here," she said, her voice echoing through their helmet comm system.

Jacen hurried forward with Tenel Ka and Lowie to see delicate crystalline growths sprouting like feathers made of ice chips. Transparent needles branched in random directions, beautiful and glistening in the glow from Jaina's helmet light.

"What are they?" Jacen said, breathless with wonder. "Are they alive?"

"Some kind of silicon formation," his sister answered.

"Ah. Aha," Tenel Ka said. "Crystal ferns. I have heard of them in other asteroids. Some prospectors search for them. They are quite fragile and therefore are considered great treasures."

"Should we take one of those for Mom?" Jacen asked.

"No, let them keep growing," Jaina said. "I want something more . . . special. Something less fragile." She hopped across the broad fissure, but misjudged the low gravity and ended up flying many meters beyond the edge.

"Hey, that looks like fun." Jacen took a flying leap and soared over his sister's head, tumbling in the air, and then gradually drifted back down to the surface.

"Be careful," Jaina said. "It wouldn't take too much to reach escape velocity on this little rock—you'd fly off into space, and we'd have to go through the trouble of capturing you again."

"Oh," Jacen said. "I guess that would be something to avoid."

Jaina found a polished lake of pure solidified metal and knelt down, pulling her lightsaber free from its clip at her belt. "Looks like a good spot," she said.

She switched on the lightsaber and scribed a rough octagon in the surface, cutting deep and angling toward the center. Tenel Ka and Lowie went to help. The pure metal vaporized, sizzling and popping in the cold vacuum as Jaina worked with slow precision to cut free a piece of what had once been the core of Alderaan.

While his sister continued her careful excavation, Jacen went to look at a series of small holes no wider than his leg punched into the surface of the asteroid. He ducked down, shining his helmet beacon into one of the deep round craters.

When his light gleamed on an open mouth and set of sharp teeth, he stumbled backward with a panicked cry. "Blaster bolts!" Just then, something lunged out—long and snakelike, with a body like a fat worm and a mouth that held much more than its share of teeth.

In the low gravity Jacen's quick reaction sent him tumbling backward, end over end. When he finally righted himself, he saw a larval space slug still thrashing and snapping for victims, rooted inside its little crater tunnel.

"Friend Jacen, are you all right?" Tenel Ka had bounded over immediately upon hearing his outcry through their helmet comm systems.

"Just surprised, that's all." He gestured with a gloved hand toward the writhing space slug. "I didn't expect anything *alive* out here—we're in open space and hard vacuum."

Jaina came over, laughing more with relief that her brother was safe than from any outright mirth.

Jacen took a deep breath. "Dad told us that when he and Mom were in the Hoth asteroid belt, what they thought was a cave turned out to be the gullet of a huge space slug. Those creatures are rare, though— I've never seen one before. Especially not a baby."

Curious, he crept forward to look at the specimen as it withdrew slowly back into its hole. "This must be a young one. They feed on metal, I think, so this core asteroid would be a good place to raise larvae."

Tenel Ka agreed gruffly. "The asteroid would provide nourishment for a very long time."

As Jacen bent closer, his light startled the young space slug, and it lunged out again, snapping its teeth. The creature seemed blind, unable to locate its exact target. Jacen backed off. "I guess it doesn't want to be disturbed," he said dejectedly.

Jaina returned to her work and a few moments later lifted out a beautiful solid chunk. The heavy metallic prize glittered and shone in the soft light. The lightsaber cutting had given it polished sides and clean edges, so that the metal looked like a bright faceted gem.

"All right, we've got what we came for," she said, delight and excitement pouring through her voice. "We promised Dad we'd head right home."

The young Jedi Knights followed her back to the *Rock Dragon*, and Jacen cast one brief glance toward where the space slug had gone back to its lair.

Inside the ship again, their suits removed, Jacen powered up the comm system to send a message to Yavin 4. Raynar answered the signal, apparently assigned to communication duties again at the Jedi academy. "Hey, Raynar," Jacen said, "we just wanted to report in."

"Good. Han Solo's been in here a dozen

times, waiting to hear from you," Raynar
said. "He's getting anxious."

Jacen laughed. "You can tell Dad that we
found what we wanted. Our mission is a
complete success."

"I'll tell him that," the young man from
Alderaan said. "You're being very mysterious."

"Well, we *are* on sort of a secret mission,
you know," Jacen said with a grin. He
signed off and sat back in his chair as the
others fastened their crash webbing and
Jaina powered up the *Rock Dragon*'s engines.

Time to go back to Yavin 4, before anything went wrong. . . .

14

WHILE JAINA SAT back, polishing and admiring the chunk of metal she had taken from Alderaan's core, Lowbacca took the pilot's seat of the *Rock Dragon*, piloting them through the hazards of the asteroid belt.

"Just take us home, Lowie," Jaina said. "I can't wait until we give this to Mom. I think it'll be the best present we've ever given her."

The young Wookiee growled happily, and Em Teedee translated. "Master Lowbacca comments that the piloting task you requested is certainly within his capabilities and he is ready and willing to perform it."

Jaina laughed. "I thought he just said, 'Okay.'" Em Teedee gave a miffed bleep.

Lowbacca tested the ship's systems, scanning the unfamiliar Hapan controls as he powered up the engines. Carefully, he released the *Rock Dragon*'s magnetic grip on the metal asteroid. The Hapan cruiser drifted free and floated out into the rubble stream that had once been Alderaan.

Checking for his best exit path, Lowie verified the orbital streams plotted on the navigation screen. He scratched his ginger-colored fur and hoped he wouldn't have to resort to so many U-turn maneuvers to depart from the rubble field. Now that the companions weren't aimlessly searching for some unknown target, charting their path back to the Jedi academy on Yavin 4 should be a simple task—or so Lowie hoped.

Just then a strange ship appeared from out of nowhere, its weapons powered up. Without warning, the enemy ship blasted at them.

The first set of high-energy bolts streaked by, heating up the edges of their shields. Luckily, because of all the space debris, Lowie had already set the shields to maximum as a simple precaution. He roared in alarm. The other young Jedi Knights cried out, trying to hold on through the concussion. Another laser blast hammered against their shields.

The Wookiee reacted quickly with his Jedi senses, yanking at the ship's propulsion controls. Reeling the *Rock Dragon* away, he employed an unorthodox strategy and shot straight up into the heart of the asteroid field.

The attacking ship fired at them again, and Lowie spun their cruiser around, jerking the ship backward, realigning their course, and firing his thrusters at maximum.

The reckless maneuvers knocked Em Teedee loose and threw him to the floor. As Jacen and Tenel Ka both scrambled to retrieve him, the little droid wailed, "We're doomed! We're doomed!"

Jaina dropped her precious shard of Alderaan and sat up in the copilot's seat, struggling to focus on the emergency at hand. "Who's firing at us?" she said, peering through the main windowport. "I can't see the ship! Didn't they send out any warning?"

Tenel Ka tossed Em Teedee up to Jaina, who plugged the droid into the navigation console.

Another laser blast burned by, narrowly missing the *Rock Dragon*. Lowie punched the accelerators, trying to gain distance.

Jacen said, "Can't say much for this guy's manners—he didn't even introduce himself before he fired." He and Tenel Ka crawled back to their seats, holding on as Lowie spun around again, flying a frantic evasive pattern.

Jaina fought with the controls, concentrating on their onboard defenses. "I can't find the armament systems," she said. "We've got to have weapons!"

Tenel Ka said, "My grandmother would have made certain we were fully armed."

"Yes, but I didn't intend to take us into battle," Jaina replied. "I haven't studied the weapons systems yet!"

Lowie snapped a comment and continued to fly, dodging through the debris—but the sleek enemy ship came close in their wake. Em Teedee said for him, "I agree with Master Lowbacca. We've no time either for target practice or to learn these systems. I suggest we retreat immediately."

"We're trying," Jaina said, her jaw tight. "But who *is* this guy? What does he want—other than to blow us into space dust."

Tenel Ka reached forward to the comm system and activated it. "Attacking ship, please identify yourself. We mean you no harm." She waited, but the other ship did not respond.

"Maybe it's one of those pirates we thought might be hiding in the asteroid field," Jacen suggested.

"You may be correct, Jacen," Tenel Ka said.

"Here, I've got some of the weapons systems on-line," Jaina said. "But this sure isn't like the *Falcon*." She punched several buttons, then fired. Her laser shots went wide. The strange-looking ship kept coming behind them, undaunted by the display of firepower.

"Small attack vessel," Jaina muttered, checking her readouts. "Fast, high-powered, and packing more weapons than I can scan . . . this guy means business!"

"Let's just hope his business isn't to add us to the rubble of Alderaan!" Jacen said.

As if in response to Jacen's comment, the enemy ship fired again, damaging their shields. The impact sent a shudder through the *Rock Dragon*'s cockpit. Red lights burned on their control panels.

With a roar, Lowie plunged into the densest part of the rubble field, squeezing between tumbling mountains of rock, huge asteroids left over from the breakup of the planet.

Jaina fired their weapons again, and

missed once more. "I should have calibrated these things . . . or at least figured out how they worked." Her hands flew over the control panels. "Too late now."

The attacker shot another time. It seemed as if he was carefully conserving his blasts. "He can't miss. Why doesn't he just blow us away?" Jacen asked.

"He certainly has the capability," Tenel Ka said. "However, our opponent seems to be targeting us precisely. Perhaps he wishes to avoid errors. Ah, aha—he hopes to disable us."

Lowie glanced down at the status report, an electronic diagram that displayed the *Rock Dragon*'s shields, and discovered that the enemy's blows had repeatedly landed in one spot. He roared, just as Jaina saw it herself. "Our engines—he's targeting our engines! He wants to board us."

Accelerating for all the engines were worth, Lowie raced toward a cluster of huge asteroids. The enormous drifting rocks were riddled with craters, cracked with gigantic fissures left over from the planetary explosion—places to hide.

Lowbacca growled softly to himself, wondering how he could dodge the enemy long enough to gain sufficient distance to drop out of sight. Even in this forest of orbiting rocks, it seemed impossible.

The other ship fired repeatedly, scoring decisive hits. Their shields buckled, and the final blow ripped open their rear starboard engine pod. The *Rock Dragon* spun out of control.

Lowie and Jaina fought to stabilize the cruiser before they careened into an asteroid. "Power's down by sixty percent," Jaina said. "We could barely outrun him before— now we've got *no* chance."

"Perhaps we do," Tenel Ka said. She crept to the armaments control panel. "I think I know what this system is for. Find a hiding place," she said, "and head there on my mark."

"What are you going to do, Tenel Ka?" Jacen said.

"Observe."

"Do be careful!" Em Teedee wailed.

The attacking ship fired again, still making no effort to communicate with them. His blow struck its target, damaging the *Rock Dragon*'s underbelly as well as their second rear engine pod—but as the blow seared against their hull plates, Tenel Ka punched a release lever.

Canisters of ionized decoy gas and

shrapnel sprayed out of their aft cargo hatch, detonating in a fireball that washed across their pursuer's screens, almost certainly blinding him.

"Now, Lowbacca!" Tenel Ka shouted.

Lowie reacted instantly, punching the controls and arcing around into the shadows behind one of the largest asteroids. Then he curved up toward another. His golden eyes scanned for a large crater, a crack into which the *Rock Dragon* could slip.

Their ship limped along, barely able to fly, but Lowie hoped he had evaded their vicious attacker long enough to hide them from view. Suddenly he saw it: a cave. With engines failing, all of their shields gone, and only a trickle of power remaining in the propulsion systems, Lowie and Jaina fought to control the bucking Hapan ship. They needed to hold the cruiser stable just long enough to descend into the opening of the crater cave.

The jagged ceiling missed scraping their hull by only a meter. Lowie had a bad moment, half-expecting the cave to grow narrower, squeezing them between rock walls—but the chamber opened up, giving them just enough room to maneuver and land.

They settled onto the rugged surface deep within a large grotto, thumping to the ground as their engines coughed and died. Rock walls surrounded them, as if the asteroid had swallowed them up entirely.

"Good hiding place, Lowie," Jaina said, patting the Wookiee on his ginger-furred shoulder.

"Yeah," Jacen said. "Either we're safe here . . . or we're trapped."

15

IN ORBIT AROUND Ennth, safe from the powerful pull of the destructive moon, Zekk docked the *Lighting Rod* against the largest of the refugee stations. From the cockpit windows, he watched the planet below shiver and gasp in its death throes.

Though he felt stunned, his heart went out to Rastur. The evacuation commander still had not rested, continuing to work at high speed even on board the ships. Zekk suspected the man kept himself busy to divert his thoughts from grief over the loss of Shinnan.

Four reconditioned cargo haulers cruised in stable orbits next to each other, high above the atmosphere. The decommissioned, lumbering containers had been declared unserviceable for interstellar transport, but they served well enough as holding tanks for the cast-off people, refugees waiting to go back to a home blasted clean by lava and groundquakes. The freighters' engines had been ripped out, and all cargo bays had been lined with bunks and cubicles to accommodate the greatest number of people. The survivors of Ennth endured. They would give up their privacy and comfort for a year before they could venture back to the surface.

Zekk remembered being a child on one of these refugee stations, how nightmarish it had seemed to him. Yet these people were willing to suffer again, as they had eight years ago and would again eight years hence, for as long as they continued to put up with the cycle of devastation.

Smaller ships flew around, supply runners continuing their ferrying duties, dropping off cargo, arranging return schedules. Now Zekk could see that while some of them had truly come to help—as Peckhum had last time—many of the traders and "expediters" were scam artists taking advantage of a difficult situation. They charged the absolute maximum for their services that the colonists could afford, and the people of Ennth had no choice but to pay. . . .

When the last straggler ships arrived safely at the refugee stations and Zekk had settled in, he went back to his quarters on

the *Lightning Rod*, having declined the
colonists' offer of an assigned bunk inside
the cramped station. Besides, he needed
rest and peace, to be away from the crowds,
away from so many people whose lives had
suffered such tragedy. He slept for a full
eleven standard hours, awakening stiff
and sore . . . but no longer exhausted, no
longer at the edge of despair.

Back on the bustling refugee station, he
made his way toward the upper levels,
taking a series of crowded turbolifts. People
moved about, chattering with each other,
discussing what they had lost and what
they had saved, already making plans for
their return to the surface of Ennth. Zekk
nodded in greeting, but did not join in their
conversation. Something disturbed him
greatly about their persistence, their
forced optimism, their blindness to the
tragedy they could have avoided—but he
could not pinpoint it.

When he finally reached the popular
observation deck of the old cargo hauler,
Zekk scanned the groups of people until he
saw Rastur standing alone, hands clasped
behind his back as he gazed out one of the
windowports. The others left the stern
man to himself, glancing sideways at him,

then murmuring sadly to each other as they looked down upon the blistering surface of Ennth. The world boiled below them.

The rigid man moved to one side and stared through a macro-telescope mounted on a stand near the observation ports. He stared for a long, long time.

Zekk came up behind him. "Is it all gone?" he said.

Rastur was not startled. "I've checked out the positions of all our cities. Newest Coast Town, Another Hopetown, Heartland Settlement. I see nothing. No sign that we were ever there. . . . Once again, it'll be a whole new world just waiting for us."

Zekk looked through the scope and saw flaming trenches of lava. Black pillars of smoke rose up through the roiling thunderclouds. As the immense moon moved away in its orbit and stopped kneading Ennth's surface, the weather would stabilize again, the rains would come, the lava would cool—and Ennth would be a clean slate, ready for the colonists again.

And again and again.

"Why do you bother?" Zekk finally asked. He clamped his lips tight as Rastur looked at him in surprise.

"What do you mean?"

"Why do you keep coming back, when you know everything will be destroyed again in less than a decade—over and over? Every time, there's so much pain, so much death, so much destruction."

"And so much renewal," Rastur added. He pointed down. "I have already begun seismic studies, mapping out a good location to build our next Hopetown. I will also choose the best spot for erecting the house Shinnan and I designed together. Maybe I'll find another wife, or maybe I'll live alone. Life goes on. We must continue to do our best."

"But *why*, when you know it's hopeless? Why not go someplace where you can live out your lives in safety, build something that will last for future generations? There are plenty of other planets."

Rastur's eyebrows knitted together. "Because this is our home," he said, as if the answer was obvious.

"Then find *another* home," Zekk said. "I've lived many different places."

"Yes, and now you've come back to Ennth," Rastur said. "It all comes back to Ennth. This is our colony. We paid for it with our blood and our sweat. We can't just abandon it."

"Even when you know more people will die in eight years?"

"And many more people will be born in eight years," Rastur said stubbornly. "On a planet with four seasons, the colonists live and work during the spring and summer and autumn, then crawl back into their shelters during the wintertime, preparing for next spring.

"We all go about our lives during the daytime and return to sleep at night, before another day begins. Ennth is just the same. We have seven and a half years of building and renewal and success, before we must retreat for a year during this time of groundquakes and volcanic eruptions. But then we come back again and rebuild and continue our lives. It is an endless cycle."

Zekk was angry now, unwilling to accept this way of thinking. "It is a *pointless* cycle," he said.

"But you are one of us, Zekk," Rastur said. "You'll understand in time. Once you see what it means to invest all of your hope and heart in a place—a *home*—you won't be able to leave so easily."

Zekk drew in a deep breath. "Then perhaps I should just leave now," he said. "I thought this planet might become my home again . . . but this isn't the kind of change I'm looking for in my life. You can have Ennth and your endless cycle. I need something more permanent."

Zekk raced away from the Ennth system in the *Lightning Rod*, not turning back to look at the bloated refugee stations or the angry moon whose gravity still ravaged the planetary surface.

He flew on, his eyes and mind grimly focused forward. He would follow the Force now—the light side—letting it direct him. He would bounce from place to place until he found his destiny.

He knew that if he trusted the Force, he couldn't go wrong.

16

IN THEIR UNCERTAIN and desperate hiding place inside the broken asteroid, Jaina shut down all of the *Rock Dragon*'s power systems, hoping to prevent detection by the enemy ship.

"First order of business is to check the extent of our damage," she said, moving about, all businesslike. She would have to keep her cool during this emergency if the young Jedi Knights were to survive. "I'm not entirely familiar with Hapan engines or electronics, but we've *got* to make these repairs."

Jacen turned to the warrior girl from Dathomir, his eyebrows raised, and leaned close to her. "Do you think your grandmother remembered to put an instruction manual in this ship?"

Tenel Ka nodded with a grim expression. "I would not be surprised if she had included specific procedures on making emergency

155

repairs in an asteroid field while an enemy hunts for this ship."

"Ta'a Chume is a very thorough lady," Jacen argued.

Jaina consulted the console sensors before switching them off to conserve their power cells. She determined that the cave contained a minimal atmosphere; it seemed thick enough that they could survive outside, provided they wore breathing masks. "Least we won't need to wear environment suits," she said. "That'll make repairs a lot easier."

"Mistress Jaina, is there anything I can do to assist you?" Em Teedee said. "I am highly capable in many forms of communication—especially in conferring with electronic devices, such as the ship's computer."

"Good idea, Em Teedee," Jaina said. "Lowie, let's hook up your little droid to the *Rock Dragon*'s diagnostic systems and see if he can find any shortcuts or reroutings we can use to bypass the damaged systems. Meanwhile, the rest of us'll check out the external damage." She placed her hands on her narrow hips. "If we get the engines up and running, we can probably make do with only a few patches on the hull plating. Our primary mission now is just getting out of here alive."

"That is a good mission," Tenel Ka agreed, fastening her breathing mask over her face. Jaina and Jacen did the same.

While Lowbacca remained inside to tinker with Em Teedee, wiring him to the control panels, the other three exited the ship. Jaina used the light of a glowrod to study the craggy rocks of the cavern ceiling. The entire asteroid had nearly split apart from the immense impact of another meteoroid that had scooped out this crater. The air was thin and cold, the floor rough, the walls jagged.

But they were probably safe for now. They just had to hope the attacking ship hadn't seen them duck into the shelter.

"Things could be worse. At least we're not inside one of those giant space slugs," Jacen said. He kicked at the rocks under his feet, then shrugged. "Hey—it never hurts to check."

Jaina flipped her straight hair behind her ears and made her way to the rear of the Hapan ship, where most of the attacker's precision shots had landed. She felt dismayed at the sight of the blackened patches and carbon-scored holes sizzled through the engine cowlings and shield plates that protected their stardrives.

Using her multitool, Jaina stripped away the charred outer debris and looked at the mangled disarray that remained of one of their drives. The second engine had fared better: still damaged but possibly reparable, given a few spare parts, a lot of intuition, and some risky rewiring.

She pointed to the burned metal plating and destroyed components. "Jacen, Tenel Ka—while I check with Lowie to see what diagnostics Em Teedee's been able to run, I'd like you two to dismantle these damaged systems. Pull them out—we'll have to bypass them. Maybe we can salvage a cyberfuse or two . . . but they look pretty slagged to me."

"That was going to be my expert opinion," Jacen said.

Inside the *Rock Dragon*'s cockpit, Jaina bent over Em Teedee where Lowbacca had hardwired him into the main control systems.

"This is all terribly confusing," the translating droid said, his optical sensors glowing up from the center of the cockpit panels. "At first I found all this Hapan engineering to be completely incomprehensible. However, as I continue to study these systems, I believe I'm beginning to understand. I *am* gifted with self-learning capabilities, you know."

Lowie pointed out the displayed schematics, gesturing with his furry arms and making suggestions. Since he was preoccupied with the ship's complex systems, Em Teedee couldn't spare the computing power to translate the Wookiee words, but Jaina could figure out most of what Lowie meant. "You want us to divert all the power from our weapons systems and shunt it into our remaining engine? You think that's smart?"

This comment finally got Em Teedee's attention. "But Master Lowbacca, that would leave us completely defenseless!"

Lowie made a sharp comment, and Jaina knew what the young Wookiee meant. If the attacking ship found them before they could escape, they'd all be doomed anyway—with or without weapons.

"I agree. We'll have to put everything we can into our engines," Jaina said with a sigh. "Let's get them repaired, plot an immediate path through hyperspace, and head off on that vector. I just hope we can jump to lightspeed before that pirate locks on to us and shoots us down."

Lowie groaned his agreement, and Em Teedee refrained from comment. Jaina knew they would all have to work together, and quickly. She guessed that the other ship was still combing the rubble field, ready to blast them to pieces. He must have intended to capture the young Jedi Knights at first, targeting carefully—but now they had eluded him. Any inexperienced pilot might have been fooled by Tenel Ka's trick of the exploding gas canisters, but Jaina couldn't imagine *this* adversary would be so easily deceived . . . whoever he was.

With Em Teedee wired into the main controls, Jaina and Lowie worked outside to reconfigure the ship's weaponry, routing the power through the remaining engine. The *Rock Dragon* carried a respectable supply of parts for emergency repairs, but no spare engines. The starboard drive was a total loss, providing only a few minor components and connections they could use in their repairs. Biting her lower lip, Jaina refused to give in to despair. She would just have to be resourceful.

Jacen and Tenel Ka offered their assistance, and followed instructions from the two mechanically inclined Jedi trainees. It reminded Jaina of the efforts the companions had made when fixing Qorl's crashed TIE fighter in the jungles—but this time their labors were not just for their amusement. They needed to repair the *Rock Dragon* for their very survival.

"Hey," Jacen said, trying to lighten the mood, "what did the new animal trainer say after his first day of working with a team of vicious battle dogs?" He paused a beat. "This job is a *pain in the nek*!" He looked around, waiting for a response. "Uh . . . get it? They're called *nek* battle dogs, you see, and—oh, never mind."

As the hours passed and the four friends worked together without complaint, Jacen and Lowie grew more and more convinced that they had escaped their enemy, that the hiding place in the crater cave had been a superb choice. Jaina did not share their optimism. She felt a growing dread that every passing minute brought their pursuer closer to discovering them. . . .

"I guess that's the best we can do," she finally said, slamming shut the clumsily repaired access panel. She hoped the engines and power sources would hold together long enough to haul the ship away.

Lowie grumbled a comment, but without Em Teedee they couldn't get an exact translation.

Jacen offered, "I think he said this ship isn't going to withstand too much bouncing around." The Wookiee chuffed and nodded.

"This is a fact," Tenel Ka said, "but Hapan technology is often sturdier than it might look."

"Well, what are we waiting for?" Jaina said with a sigh, taking a final glance at their uncertain repairs.

They climbed back inside the *Rock Dragon*, subdued. All four of them knew the gamble they had decided to take.

Seated in the pilot's chair, Jaina powered up the systems with nervous fingers. The engines thrummed, vibrating with power, stuttering and popping, but the output held. Jaina bit her lower lip and sensed the flow through the engines, the pulse through the ship.

The *Rock Dragon* trembled, humming unsteadily. The ship felt sick to Jaina, not up to its normal peak levels. But it would fly, and that was all they needed.

She glanced over at Lowbacca. He smoothed down the dark streak of fur on his forehead, then nodded at her. Lowie activated the repulsorlifts, and the ship raised up off the rocky floor in the low gravity.

"All systems go," Jaina said.

"All right!" Jacen cheered. "We're on our way."

Tenel Ka sat gripping the edge of her seat with her hand, leaning slightly toward Jacen. The ship moved forward, approaching the narrow passageway through the rocks.

Still wired into the console, Em Teedee said, "I can confirm that our escape path lies directly through that opening. I must say that this ship has superb sensors. In fact, I can even detect—*oh, dear!*"

Before the translating droid could sound an alarm, as Jaina gently maneuvered the *Rock Dragon* through the narrow passageway toward open space, the silhouette of the enemy ship appeared at the mouth of the cave. Its laser cannons already glowed brightly.

"He's found us!" Jacen cried just as the other ship opened fire.

Wrenching the controls, Jaina hoped to reverse their engines and evade the blast, but this time their enemy did not target the *Rock Dragon* itself. Instead, its powerful lasers pulverized the unstable roof of the crater cave.

The ceiling collapsed. Boulders split off from precarious positions, and the entire avalanche tumbled in slow motion, pounding down on the ship like sledgehammers . . . burying them within the empty cave.

17

FALLING BOULDERS SOUNDED like thunder outside the *Rock Dragon*. All the ship's systems went dark, plunging them into blackness.

Buried alive.

Jaina braced herself at the controls, but knew she could do nothing—not yet.

Gradually, backup systems kicked in. Em Teedee, working frantically to tap into their emergency power, restored a low glow to illuminate the cabin of the Hapan passenger cruiser.

Jaina's head ached, but she drove away thoughts of pain as she got to her feet to make sure her friends were all right. As soon as the lights flickered back on, she swept her gaze over the others. Lowbacca, Jacen, and Tenel Ka all appeared to be stunned but uninjured.

Jaina scrambled back into her seat, suppressing a groan. "Em Teedee, is our hull integrity still intact?" She rubbed her left temple. "Any leakage?"

"Oh, Mistress Jaina! The diagnostic systems have simply gone mad," the little droid wailed. "This is terribly distressing. Why, I—"

"Em Teedee," she snapped, "are we leaking air or not?"

"No, Mistress Jaina—we seem to be intact."

Jacen, who lay on the floor of the cockpit, snorted and ran his fingers through his tousled hair. "I'll bet we wouldn't win any prizes for best-maintained ship in the galaxy," he said. He moaned. "Guess I should've buckled my crash webbing before we started to move, huh?"

"Prizes for ship maintenance are not our concern at the moment," Tenel Ka answered, offering her hand to help him to his feet.

"Looks like we'll have to make some of the same repairs again," Jaina said, scanning the other cockpit systems. "And a few new ones, too. I wonder if that other ship has given us up for dead."

"I hope so," Jacen said. "Then he'd just leave, wouldn't he?"

Tenel Ka shook her head. "No, I believe his strategy was to trap us, not to kill. He wants something from us . . . though he refuses to communicate directly."

Rigged up at the control panels, Em Teedee let out a bleep of surprise. "Oh, alarm! Alarm! Emergency! Dear me, this is dreadful!"

"What is it, Em Teedee?" Jaina said, swivelling in the pilot's chair to look at him. "A hull breach?"

"No, I can't bear it! We are being violated—scanned! Someone is copying everything in our memory banks."

"Scanned? How can anyone scan us? That would take a . . ."

"Indeed, it is a remote slicer, Mistress Jaina—a highly illegal piece of equipment, if my memory circuits are functioning properly. I should think he'd be ashamed!"

"I guess he hasn't given us up for dead, then," Jacen said.

Lights flashed on the control panels as the enemy ship linked up to their computers, skimming through their files. "If he reads our navigation history and our ship's log entries," Tenel Ka said, "he will know who we are."

Scrambling with the controls, Jaina and Lowie were unable to block their enemy's computer access probe. "Not a thing we can do about it, either," Jaina said. Lowie growled.

"Well, we would have introduced ourselves by now, if he'd just given us the chance," Jacen said.

Jaina pounded on the control panel in frustration. She seemed to be entirely out of options. "I don't believe this! Remote slicers are completely illegal—not to mention expensive. Never even seen one myself. Only the most powerful high rollers can afford them."

"Of course," Tenel Ka said, raising her eyebrows and tossing her head to fling her reddish-gold braids behind her, "a certain powerful high roller helped to outfit *this* ship—and my grandmother always plans for many . . . contingencies."

Jacen, Jaina, and Lowie all looked at her, comprehension dawning on their faces.

"Em Teedee," Jaina said breathlessly, "see if the *Rock Dragon* has one of those remote slicers."

"But Mistress Jaina, there is such an

unusual combination of systems on board that I—"

"Just check, Em Teedee!"

"Yes, very well," the little droid said. "Amazing! Why, I do believe I have found one. I'm quite astonished, since upstanding citizens could hardly be expected to deal in such illegal and unorthodox equipment."

"That means we can use our *own* remote transmitter to pull data from our friend's memory banks, see who he is and what he's after," Jaina said, feeling her heart pound with new optimism. "Turnabout. Give this guy a taste of his own medicine."

"Shall I begin now, Mistress Jaina?" Em Teedee said hopefully. "I'm certain I can perform the appropriate slicing functions. I feel so . . . useful here in my position. Almost like the captain of a ship."

"Don't get delusions of grandeur, Em Teedee," Jacen said, and Lowie chuffed with laughter.

"Using the *Rock Dragon*'s remote slicer would not be a wise idea at the moment," Tenel Ka said. "If we did, our enemy would know we were alive—and that we had background information—just as we can see he's probing us now."

"Good point," Jaina said. "Wait a while,

Em Teedee. Meantime, we should go out and check over our situation, move a few rocks, see how bad it is this time."

"Yeah," Jacen said, "before our friend figures out what to do with the information he's stolen from us."

Carrying portable high-powered glow-rods, the young Jedi Knights put on their breathing masks and ventured out into the collapsed cavern to look over the battered exterior of the ship. Rock shards had pounded the *Rock Dragon*'s hull, smashing the already-damaged engines, the stabilizers, and some of the external communications systems.

"We're banged up—but it could have been a lot worse," Jacen said optimistically.

"The Force was with us," Tenel Ka said.

Lowie groaned and gestured toward what had been the opening of the crater cave. A collapsed wall of rock completely blocked the exit. Boulders piled in a jumbled wall sealed them inside like a tomb. The Wookiee's shoulders slumped.

Jaina patted his ginger-furred arm. "With our lightsabers and the Force, I'm sure we can clear that away . . . given time."

"But how much time do you think we have?" Jacen said. Nobody hazarded a guess.

Jaina cleared the rubble from the top of the ship and climbed up onto it. Kneeling, she inspected the hull plates, brushing away dust with her fingertips. "Like Em Teedee said, no evident ruptures. The worst news, though, is that our communications array is smashed. We can't send out a distress signal."

"Not that we'd want to," Jacen said.

"My friend Jacen is correct," Tenel Ka said. "A distress signal would only lure others into the ambush. We do not know how many more pirates may be hiding in this asteroid field."

"There's already one too many," Jacen said. Bending over, he hefted one of the boulders that had wedged itself between a flight fin and a starboard stabilizer, and tossed it aside. The young man grinned as he saw the rock fly farther than he had anticipated in the asteroid's low gravity. "Hey, it's easier than it looks!"

"I wish we knew who our enemy is, and

why he shot us down," Jaina said. "Maybe it's all a mistake."

Then they whirled as blasting sounds came from the rubble wall that had sealed them into the cramped chamber.

Lowbacca growled, his fur fluffing in anger as he bared his fangs.

"Our enemy has come for us," Tenel Ka said.

"Blaster bolts—we left our lightsabers in the ship!" Jacen cried.

Stone shards exploded into powder at the center of the avalanche wall. Then, as the smoke settled and the incinerated rock cooled, a figure stepped through the opening, holding his blaster out and ready to fire. He wore scratched armor and a helmet like the ancient Mandalorian warriors had once used.

Boba Fett.

"Children of Han Solo," the bounty hunter said in a gruff, threatening voice.

Jaina sucked in a shocked breath. "My father told us about you," she said, straightening to kneel on one knee on top of the ship. She crossed her arms over her chest. "Why have you attacked us? There's no bounty on our ship."

"Hey, there's not even a bounty on our *dad* anymore," Jacen added.

"I am not hunting Han Solo," Fett answered. "I have moved on to other assignments. Where is Bornan Thul?"

Bornan Thul? Jaina couldn't understand why the bounty hunter would be interested in Raynar's father, or why Fett had attacked *them* to get that information.

"Bornan Thul! How would *we* know where he is?" Jacen said.

"I intercepted your transmission to his son. You reported that your mission was a complete success. Since Bornan Thul was a noble of Alderaan, it makes sense that he might have chosen to hide here. You must have come here to meet him. Where is the man, and where is his cargo? I must find him."

"Well, happy hunting then," Jaina said, scowling. "We don't know where he is, and that's not at all why we came to this system."

"Now will you let us go?" Jacen asked.

"You will be bait, then," Fett said. "Perhaps Han Solo knows where Bornan Thul has gone."

"No!" Jaina cried. Lowie growled.

The armored bounty hunter turned,

strode through the small opening he had blasted through the rock wall. Before he disappeared back to his own ship, the bounty hunter fired his blaster at the roof of the small tunnel, bringing down a new rock slide and fusing its core.

"Not very talkative, is he?" Jacen said.

Tenel Ka looked around, an expression of deep concern on her face. "Who would set a bounty on Raynar's father—and why?"

"And why would he want us as bait?" Jacen asked.

"If he sends out a fake message, he'll lure Dad here into an ambush," Jaina said. "Unless we can get out first. Come on!"

Back inside their ship, the miniaturized translating droid was immensely pleased to see them. "I have excellent news, Mistress Jaina and Master Lowbacca! When I realized that dreadful bounty hunter was outside with you, I took the opportunity to use our remote slicer to tap into his computer." Em Teedee seemed immensely pleased with himself. "I assumed he wouldn't notice, since he was no longer aboard his ship. I've succeeded in retrieving all of his data files!"

"Great work, Em Teedee!" Jacen said. Lowie made an appreciative noise and patted the droid's silvery external shell with his big hairy hand.

"Good," Jaina said. "Now that we have Boba Fett's information, maybe we can find a way to get out of this alive."

18

"I'M IMPRESSED, EM Teedee," Jacen said, still marveling at the little droid's audacity.

"Why, thank you, Master Jacen. It was nothing so remarkable, really." Jacen was sure the little droid would have blushed had he been able to. "Oh—dear me! I seem to be picking up a broadband transmission from *Slave IV,* Boba Fett's ship. It's being sent on a wide range of frequencies."

"Put it through our speakers," Jaina ordered.

"Reception is rather weak, thanks to our damaged communications dish, but I'll amplify as much as possible," Em Teedee said. Jaina and Lowie worked together to boost the gain, their fingers flying over the control panels.

The ship's speakers crackled with static. ". . . for Han Solo . . . emergency in

Alderaan system. Jacen and Jaina need help . . . urgent. Come alone."

The mood in the *Rock Dragon*'s cockpit instantly turned grim.

"I don't get it," Jacen said, feeling more trapped and anxious than he had earlier.

"Ah." Tenel Ka nodded. "Aha. Your father will naturally come if he believes you to be in danger."

Jacen clenched his fists, then looked down at his hands. "Why would Boba Fett think Dad could lead him to Bornan Thul?"

"Looks like Boba Fett knew that Dad and Bornan Thul were on the same trade commission," Jaina said, scrolling through the data Em Teedee had downloaded from the bounty hunter's ship. "Let's see what else we can find out. Maybe if we learn who Boba Fett is working for, why he wants Bornan Thul so badly . . ."

Leaning over his sister's shoulder, Jacen quickly skimmed the information that flashed across the screen. "Fett's after something, all right. I just can't tell what it is."

"That fact is never specified," Tenel Ka said.

"Seems like Raynar's dad may be the key, though," Jaina said. "Whoever posted the bounty seems to think Bornan Thul has—or at least knows where to find— whatever it is Boba Fett's after."

Lowie gave a soft rumble. "More than one *what*, Lowie?" Jaina said.

"Master Lowbacca believes that because Boba Fett has records tracking the movements of other searchers, it is likely that more than one bounty hunter was engaged to fulfill this assignment," Em Teedee clarified. "According to one log entry, he has apparently already destroyed one such rival, a man named Moorlu."

Jacen gave a low whistle. "Somebody must *really* want Raynar's father."

"Ah. Aha," Tenel Ka said, pointing to a name on the screen. "There—Nolaa Tarkona. It would appear that she set the bounty. Interesting." Jacen knew Tenel Ka expected this to mean something to him, but he had no idea what she was getting at. He gave her a blank look.

Tenel Ka raised her eyebrows. "Recall what your father told Raynar. Bornan Thul was on his way to a trade conference when he disappeared. At the conference, he was scheduled to meet with Nolaa Tarkona, a Twi'lek woman—one of the few females of that species ever to rise to political prominence. My experience with assassins and conspiracies indicates this connection is not entirely coincidental."

"Seems awfully complicated," Jacen said. "Dad's in trouble. Raynar's father is in trouble. We're in trouble. . . ."

"At least now we *know* something about the trouble we're in," Jaina said. "Thanks to this information. Excellent work, Em Teedee."

"Why, that's very kind of you, Mistress Jaina," the translating droid said. "But the credit actually belongs to you and Master Lowbacca for enhancing my emergency response subroutines. I simply—"

"Speaking of emergency response," Jaina broke in, "we'd better all get back to digging ourselves out of this mess before Dad falls into the trap Boba Fett is setting for him."

Jacen nodded. He didn't mind his sister's taking charge in a crisis. He knew Jaina didn't do it to show off—she took the lead because someone had to, and it usually just worked out that way. Jaina thought faster and felt more comfortable issuing orders than he did.

"Em Teedee, try to send a message to warn Dad away from Boba Fett's ambush. I know the signal's weak, but do whatever you can to boost it until I can get another transmitter dish rigged."

"I'll use every resource at my disposal, Mistress Jaina," Em Teedee said. "You may rely on me to do everything within my power to see that—"

"Good," Jaina cut in. "Get right on it. Lowie and I will work on the antenna dish and get the ship ready to fly again—if we can. Jacen, you and Tenel Ka go outside and see if you can get enough of that blockage cleared so we can fly the *Rock Dragon* out of here. Moving a little mountain of rock shouldn't be too hard if you two work together."

Jacen groaned, but Tenel Ka gripped his shoulder. "We will do whatever is necessary to get the job done. If Boba Fett believes us to be permanently trapped, I will be pleased to prove him wrong."

"He probably doesn't know we can use the Force," Jacen pointed out. "It won't be much harder for us than helping Uncle Luke clear rubble at the Great Temple. Of course, we won't have all the other Jedi students to help. . . ."

"We will clear the way," Tenel Ka said confidently. "Our muscles can do much of the work. The Force will do the rest."

Jacen and Tenel Ka hastily put on their breathing masks and tough, flexible gloves. Full of determination, they stepped out into the thin, cold atmosphere of the darkened cave. But when they turned on their glowrods and approached the mounded blockage, Jacen's spirits fell. The central core of the debris where Boba Fett had fired his blaster to reseal the cave was fused into a solid rocky mass.

"Uh-oh," he said.

Tenel Ka gestured with her glowrod to the side of the cave-in, where the rock had fallen in easily manageable chunks and pebbles. Jacen moved over to the pile and experimentally hefted a chunk of rock twice the size of his head. In the low gravity, it seemed to weigh no more than a gort-feather pillow. Tenel Ka picked up a similar-sized rock with her one hand and tossed it aside with no problem.

Next they experimented with using the Force to nudge aside larger pieces of rock while shoving away mounds of loose pebbles with their gloved hands. Though the air in the cave was as frigid as a night on Hoth, they both soon worked up a sweat.

Jacen grinned at Tenel Ka, feeling a bit silly for enjoying himself so much—but he did like to work with the warrior girl from Dathomir. He found it inexplicably satisfying to be struggling with his friends to solve a problem. They would get themselves out of this mess—he had no doubt of that.

Jacen even started trying to concoct a joke: How many Jedi does it take to clear an asteroid cave-in? He might have to wait until after they got back home, he supposed, to find the right punch line.

When they had opened an area a meter deep beside the fused stone core, Tenel Ka climbed atop the rubble and withdrew her rancor-tooth lightsaber. Then, igniting the brilliant turquoise blade, she used it like a battle-ax to hack off a massive wedge of rock. Jacen caught the slab with the Force and diverted it quickly to one side while Tenel Ka sliced off another wedge, as if she were manipulating a machete to chop her way through a dense jungle.

She gave Jacen an approving nod, and he knew he had been right: they would get out of this just fine.

"Thanks, Lowie," Jaina said, accepting the mangled wreckage of what had once been their transmitter dish. The Wookiee had just dismantled it from the battered roof of the *Rock Dragon*, then hauled it inside the cockpit where Jaina could work on it. Parts of the dish were missing entirely, pulverized in the avalanche, but more than half of the contraption had survived—in some form. Fixing it would be the difficult part.

"I'll see what I can do with this. Navigation systems, life support, and hyperdrive all checked out fine. I think I've got the engine fixed again. Can you run a diagnostic on all our exhaust ports and make sure they're not clogged with debris?"

Lowie roared his agreement. "Please be careful, Master Lowbacca," Em Teedee called from the control console. "Did you know that twenty-one percent of all spaceport accidents occur while attempting to clear blockage to exhaust ports?"

Lowie grumbled reassuringly and headed toward the rear of the ship.

Kneeling down, Jaina ran a grim eye over the twisted remains of the *Rock Dragon*'s transmitter dish. "I'm not even sure there's enough here left to salvage." She sighed.

"Perhaps you might consider fashioning a smaller transmitter from the remains of the old one," Em Teedee said.

Jaina bit her lower lip and looked dubiously at the mangled components. "I'm pretty sure I can do that," she said. "The question is, will it still be strong enough to send a signal? We have to warn Dad about the ambush."

"I have the utmost confidence in your abilities, Mistress Jaina," Em Teedee said encouragingly.

"Yeah?" Jaina sighed again. "Well, then, don't complain if I have to disassemble you for spare parts."

"I should hope that I could be of greater use to you as one complete unit," the little droid said. "Actually, because my own modest transmitter is fully integrated, I doubt—"

"That's it!" Jaina said, slapping her palm to her forehead. "The modular transmitter Dad brought me. It's old, but I just may be able to rig something." She grinned at Em Teedee. "Don't worry, Quicksilver, your parts are safe. I knew we kept you around for a good reason."

19

WITH THE STONES and debris finally cleared from the mouth of the cave, and knowing that Boba Fett lurked somewhere out in the rubble field, waiting for Han Solo, the young Jedi Knights prepared the *Rock Dragon* for a last desperate dash toward freedom.

Jaina sat in the pilot's seat, frowning and tense as she checked the control readouts for the tenth time.

"What we really need is a Mon Calamari star cruiser for what we're about to do," Jacen said, looking over at his sister.

"This is a fact," Tenel Ka said, "but Master Skywalker taught us that a Jedi makes use of the skills she possesses—not the resources she *wishes* she had."

"Well, here we go." Jaina fired up the *Rock Dragon*'s repulsorjets, and the battered ship rose, blasting rock dust from the floor and walls. More pebbles trickled down, bouncing and sliding as the engine vibrations shook the asteroid. "Hang on."

"Be careful," Jacen said. "That hole we carved isn't going to be very stable. It could collapse at any minute."

Jaina shrugged. "So there's no point in sticking around any longer." She looked over at the Wookiee in the copilot's seat. "Punch it, Lowie."

Taking a deep breath, Jacen readied himself at the comm system, prepared to send his warning message the moment they burst free from the shielding rock walls. Once they were out of the cavern, even their weak jury-rigged transmitter should send a discernible signal. He knew their father might already be on his way to rescue them—and that Boba Fett would be waiting to ambush the *Millennium Falcon*.

With its meager engine power and its sublight drives strained to the maximums, the *Rock Dragon* shot through the broken opening. Perspiration rolling down her face, Jaina gripped the controls, entirely focused in her concentration. They pulled free of the asteroid's weak gravity and launched themselves headlong into space.

"Now, Jacen," she said through gritted teeth. "Send the signal!"

Jacen flicked on the comm system, transmitting on all bands. "Warning to incoming craft! This is Jacen Solo on the *Rock Dragon*. The bounty hunter Boba Fett is waiting in ambush. He has attacked us and will shoot down anyone who comes into the Alderaan rubble field. We are in desperate need of assistance—but beware of traps."

"Our enemy has found us," Tenel Ka announced.

Like a combat arachnid waiting for prey, Boba Fett's angular ship spun out from where it had been hiding in the eclipsing shadow of another asteroid. The *Slave IV* rocketed after them. The bounty hunter again made no attempt at communication, but Jacen could sense the danger.

"I think he's mad at us," he said. "D'you suppose he knows we tapped into his computer?"

"I'm afraid I didn't precisely attempt to cover my intrusion," Em Teedee said. "Was I supposed to?"

As if in answer to the little droid's question, Boba Fett blasted with his laser cannons, flaming through their shields, damaging the *Rock Dragon*'s hull plates. He fired with no finesse this time—just brute force. It seemed that he was through playing games.

"There goes our one good chance," Jaina said in dismay. "He's not just targeting our engines—he means to slag us."

"Oh, my—what *are* we to do?" Em Teedee cried.

Lowie growled about having no weapons as he frantically scrambled with the controls. Jacen didn't want to know the details.

"I think we're out of options," Jaina said. "We bypassed all our attack systems, and we can't fight against his laser cannons."

"I have an alternative." Tenel Ka took a deep breath and said grimly, "We can *ram* him."

"Let's think of a different option," Jaina replied, wrestling with the controls to avoid crashing into an asteroid as they dodged the bounty hunter's attack. "I'm open to suggestions."

Boba Fett fired again, clearly intent on destroying them this time. Their shields had failed, and the burning energy of Fett's laser blasts blew up their newly repaired port stardrive. The starboard engine remained off line from the first attack.

The *Rock Dragon* shuddered and fell

dead, coasting in space with nothing but its altitude-control jets for maneuvering. Most of their power systems went out, along with life-support generators. Alarm lights flashed and sirens blared, and Em Teedee suffered several short circuits just trying to process them all.

"We're dead in space," Jaina said. "This is it."

"Dad's not going to get here in time, is he?" Jacen said. "And there's no one else to help us."

He looked over at Tenel Ka, wanting to say so much as he stared into her cool gray eyes, which were wide open and filled with the many things that she in turn apparently wanted to say to him.

"Hey, been nice knowing you," Jacen told her, forcing a lopsided grin.

In the asteroid field, Boba Fett's bounty ship circled the helpless target, coming around for the kill shot. All of his laser cannons powered up, bright points of light ready to fire.

Boba Fett spun the *Slave IV* around, heading straight toward his new victims.

They had surprised him with their ingenuity. Given virtually no resources or training, they had freed themselves from the avalanche and repaired their ship. But if they thought they could escape from him . . . then they were much mistaken. He would never allow them to warn Bornan Thul.

If he meant to keep from alerting his quarry to the pursuit, he could not let these others escape with the knowledge they had stolen from his computer banks. He had immediately discovered their scanning and slicing, of course, and they would have to pay the price. No one could hold that much information about Boba Fett and live.

His gauntleted hands squeezed the controls, centering the battered *Rock Dragon* in his targeting sights. His weapons powered up to full strength.

The young Jedi Knights had spoiled his ambush plans and warned Han Solo . . . but Boba Fett was flexible. All good bounty hunters were flexible. He would destroy this small passenger cruiser and cripple the *Millennium Falcon* as soon as it arrived, then proceed with the next step in his hunt for Bornan Thul.

He increased his speed, diving toward the *Rock Dragon*, then nudged the targeting controls in his weapons systems.

He placed his thumbs over the firing buttons, waiting until exactly the right moment. . . .

And then fired.

Jacen shielded his eyes, waiting for the final blast to come—but just as the bounty hunter took his shot, another ship streaked past at high speed, a clunky-looking freighter cobbled together from dozens of obsolete components.

"The *Lightning Rod*!" Jaina cried.

Old Peckhum's former ship used a tractor beam to grab the *Slave IV* and yank it off course, spinning it away just as Fett fired. The deadly laser bolts flew haphazardly into empty space, one of them striking and vaporizing a small asteroid.

"It's Zekk," Jaina said. "He found us."

The *Lightning Rod* took advantage of the element of surprise and whirled about, hammering down on Boba Fett's ship, which was still spinning out of control from the tractor beam. Zekk unleashed five rapid laser blasts from the *Lightning Rod*'s newly installed weapons systems—a precaution Peckhum had agreed to only after being shot down by Shadow Academy fighters. The blasts pounded the *Slave IV*, sending it reeling under the sudden barrage. Knowing that the *Rock Dragon* had no functional weapons systems, Boba Fett had not been expecting an attack from any direction.

"Oh, thank the maker, we're saaaaved!" Em Teedee said, his voice slightly slurred from the numerous short circuits he had recently suffered.

Apparently finding himself damaged and possibly even outgunned, Fett turned about, ignited his engines, and flew away into the labyrinth of the asteroid field, where he could hide and do repairs.

"I can't believe it—Zekk came to rescue us!" Jaina said, absolutely elated. "Jacen, get on the comm system. We've got to talk to him."

But as she watched in dismay, the *Lightning Rod* roared past them and continued in its flight, pursuing Boba Fett. Zekk kept firing, but the *Slave IV*'s more powerful engines rapidly stretched out the distance. Still Zekk wouldn't give up. He streaked ahead and was soon lost in the complex orbital paths of the rubble field.

"Where is Zekk going?" Jaina cried. "He'll get himself killed. He may have had the element of surprise, but the *Lightning Rod* can't seriously fight against Boba Fett once he gets his systems up again."

"I sure hope Zekk comes back for us," Jacen said. "Our life support's out, and we've only got a few hours before it gets very uncomfortable in here."

Without power, and with only the backup batteries left to run their communications systems and send their automated distress call, the young Jedi Knights sat and waited.

And waited.

All alone in space.

20

THE *ROCK DRAGON* drifted powerless in space among the shards of Alderaan. Jaina bit her lower lip and stared out the front viewport, her mind temporarily numb. Her thoughts seemed as unable to function as the ship's blasted control systems.

"We're dooooomed," Em Teedee said in a warbling, distorted voice. "Doooooomed."

"Hang in there, Quicksilver," Jaina said, trying to sound calm and reassuring. "We're not done for yet." She turned to look at Jacen and Tenel Ka.

"Think Boba Fett's gone for good?" she asked. Her voice came out strained and raspy. "Why doesn't Zekk come back?"

"I sense that the bounty hunter has withdrawn," Tenel Ka answered, "but I cannot be certain how far or for how long."

"Hey, are *all* bounty hunters this persistent?" Jacen asked.

Lowie gave a low woof.

"Since Master Lowbacca's experience with members of that unsavory profession is extremely limited, he has very little data on which to base an assessment of the personal attributes of bounty hunters," Em Teedee translated, though Jaina had been perfectly capable of understanding Lowie's comment, which might have been more directly translated as, "I don't know," or "Beats me."

A plaintive growl issued from the young Wookiee as he tried in vain to access any of the *Rock Dragon*'s controls. He checked out the heat and air remaining in their ship, now that the life-support systems had been deactivated.

Jaina prodded herself back into action. "Jacen, Tenel Ka, see if you can hail the *Lightning Rod*."

"We've been trying," Jacen said. "So has Em Teedee. So far, no response—not to direct signals, not to our automatic distress beacon."

Jaina felt her gut clench, fearing that Boba Fett might well have rounded on the *Lightning Rod*, fired a retaliatory blast . . . and possibly destroyed Zekk.

"Much of our equipment is malfunctioning," Tenel Ka pointed out. "We suffered severe hits, and our transmitter repairs were makeshift and unreliable at best."

Jaina knew that her friend was trying to keep her from thinking about Zekk. They all had enough problems without adding another worry. "What do you say, Lowie?" she asked. "Can we fix the ship without landing somewhere?"

"Oh no, not again," Jacen muttered.

Lowie shook his shaggy head and rumbled a discouraging report on the damage the *Rock Dragon* had sustained during battle. Em Teedee heartily agreed from where he was hardwired into the control systems. Jaina's heart sank. The situation sounded impossible.

But Jaina had promised her father they would get back to Yavin 4. Han Solo had trusted in their resourcefulness, and she wasn't about to give up without a fight.

"Well," she said with forced cheerfulness, "we're Jedi trainees, and it's time to prove just how much Master Luke has taught us. Besides, we have another thing to thank your grandmother for, Tenel Ka—a plentiful supply of spare parts."

"This is a fact," Tenel Ka said.

"Except parts for the transmitter," Jacen

reminded them glumly. "And there aren't any spare engines."

"Oh, my!" Em Teedee said. "I seem to be receiving another transmission—but I can't make any sense of it. The words don't translate well in my language data banks. I do hope it's not another bounty hunter— if it is, I'm afraid we're done for."

"Put it on speaker," Jaina said tersely.

Instantly she heard a delighted whoop, and a loud "Yeee-haa!" resounded through the cockpit, accompanied by a wordless Wookiee roar. "Kids, this is the *Millennium Falcon* comin' in for a little inspection. I got your warning, and we're ready for anything. Do you read me, *Rock Dragon?*"

"Dad!" Jaina yelled. "We're fine, but we sure need some help."

"That's no bounty hunter, Em Teedee," Jacen laughed.

"I'm only getting your distress beacon, *Rock Dragon*," Han Solo's voice came over the speaker again, "and it's pretty weak." He was interrupted by a couple of loud Wookiee barks. "Right, Chewie," Han said. "We've got you on visual now. Here we come."

After a moment, they saw the familiar shape of the *Falcon* approach, its pronged metal disk arrowing through the rocky debris. "Hey, looks like you took some pretty heavy hits to your engines. We're going to take the liberty of towing you to one of the larger asteroids to make repairs."

A tractor beam locked on to the Hapan passenger cruiser, and the ship lurched. "We've got ya—just sit tight."

After a few moments of joyous greetings between Han, Chewie, and the young Jedi Knights on the asteroid, they quickly got down to business making the much-needed repairs to the damaged passenger cruiser.

"How did you know to come after us, Dad?" Jaina asked. "You got here so fast."

Han shrugged one shoulder and studied the damage to the *Rock Dragon*'s repulsor-jets. "When you didn't make it back to Yavin 4 after three days, like you promised, I figured you were trying to collect half the planet of Alderaan and reassemble it for your mom's birthday. She's due at the Jedi academy any day now, and I didn't want to wait any longer. I guessed you might need some help."

"So it wasn't Boba Fett's message that lured you here?" Jacen asked.

"Naw, we didn't even get that until we dropped out of hyperspace, but your warning put us on our guard." He smiled and glanced at Chewie. "We still know a thing or two about evading bounty hunters."

Jaina swallowed hard. "I sure hope Zekk does. He followed Boba Fett after our fight, and we haven't heard from him since."

Han Solo gave his daughter a sympathetic look. "I'm sure he's fine, Jaina."

"I wish *I* were so sure," Jaina said, feeling despair creep up on her.

Her father raised a hand to point at something over her left shoulder. "Well, maybe you'll believe your own eyes—unless I miss my guess, that's the *Lightning Rod* coming in for a landing right now."

Though Zekk stood stiffly and uncertainly, Jaina gave the dark-haired boy a quick hug as soon as he stepped out of the *Lightning Rod*. He blushed in the dim light, then relaxed enough to hug Jaina back. They held the embrace for several seconds more.

Jacen and Han hurried over, while Chewie, Lowie, and Tenel Ka remained where they were, continuing the repairs on the *Rock Dragon.*

"We'll be safe for the moment," Zekk said, as if reluctant to step too far from his ship. "I followed Boba Fett until he dodged into hyperspace. I scored a few solid hits before his ship escaped. Don't know how much damage I caused, but I think he'll need to make some repairs himself before he tries to come back."

Han shook his head in bewilderment. "As far as I know, there aren't any bounties out on me anymore. What was Boba Fett after?"

"We're not sure," Jaina said, "but it had something to do with Raynar's father. He thought you had some information about his whereabouts. He wanted to use us as bait."

Han Solo looked surprised. "Bornan Thul? I wish I did know where to find him. Why would there be a bounty out on him? He's just a member of the trade council."

Jacen said, "Boba Fett seems to think Raynar's father knows about something that he's looking for, some sort of missing cargo."

"Em Teedee managed to slice into the *Slave IV*'s computers, so we've got a little background information," Jaina said. "Things Boba Fett probably doesn't want us to know."

"He's working for Nolaa Tarkona," Tenel Ka said.

Han gave a low whistle. "And Bornan Thul disappeared right when he was supposed to meet with her at that trade council. I thought that Twi'lek woman might've been behind his disappearance, but it doesn't sound like she knows where he is either."

"We think Nolaa Tarkona hired more than one bounty hunter to go out and look for him," Jacen said.

Han nodded. "And Boba Fett's the best bounty hunter there is."

"Maybe the best—until now," Zekk said. He had been quiet, absorbing information. Han's eyebrows went up, and he glanced curiously at the dark-haired teenager.

"What do you mean?" Jaina asked.

Zekk raised his chin. "I've been to the Jedi academy, and I don't belong there. I just went back to my home planet, Ennth, and now I'm sure that's not the place for me either. I need to go in a new direction." He glanced past the others, locking his gaze on Jaina's eyes. "So I've decided to try my hand at being . . . a bounty hunter. I plan to be the best there ever was."

Jaina bit her lower lip to stifle a gasp.

Zekk's emerald-green eyes looked earnestly into Jaina's. "I know I can't go back to the way things were, and I can't go back to who I was. We've talked about this before, Jaina. There's only one direction for me to go, and that's forward."

"Being a bounty hunter's hard work," Han pointed out. "Dangerous, too. You don't make a lot of friends."

"I have friends," Zekk said firmly. "I'm not looking to make many new ones. Besides, I still have some skills in the Force that other bounty hunters don't have. And I think I'd be good at it.

"That's how I found *you* here, you know," Zekk went on. "Jaina, remember when you told me that you were thinking of coming here, to the Alderaan rubble field? I didn't give it a second thought. But when I was drifting away from Ennth, trying to figure out where to go, letting the Force guide me, I got a strange and powerful feeling that you were in trouble. That's why I came, at the *Lightning Rod*'s top speed. Good thing, too."

He looked around, shuffling his feet uncomfortably. "Maybe as a bounty hunter I

can even find what Nolaa Tarkona is looking for before anyone else does—it would
serve Boba Fett right for trying to kill my
friends."

Jaina saw a familiar look come over
her father's face. Han Solo was intrigued.
"You know, kid, that's not a half-bad
idea. . . . I think you could be some real
help to the New Republic."

Jaina saw a spark of hope lighten Zekk's
face at this encouragement, and she knew
that she had lost any chance of persuading
him to return with her to the Jedi academy
now. But she had known that already,
hadn't she? She had only friendship to
offer him, nothing more.

Jaina sighed. Forward: there was no
other direction to go.

She cleared her throat, trying to ignore
the painful lump forming there. "My dad
knows a lot about bounty hunters and
smugglers, Zekk. He's learned plenty of
tricks over the years. Maybe he could give
you a few tips." She darted a glance at her
father to get his approval, and he gave her
a slight nod.

Zekk's brows drew together, and his emerald eyes darkened as if he were fighting
some internal battle. Then, as quickly as it

had come, the inner storm passed, and he stood straight again, his smile bright.

Zekk reached for Jaina's hand and gave it a brief squeeze. "Thanks," he said. "I'll take you up on that."

21

IT WAS LATE afternoon when the *Rock Dragon* and the *Millennium Falcon* touched down on the landing field near the Great Temple. The Hapan ship's engines still sounded weary and uneven as it descended through the humid atmosphere—but the craft flew passably, and had made it through hyperspace all the way back to Yavin 4 without a mishap.

Jacen couldn't remember the jungles of Yavin 4 ever looking greener, more full of life. The distant sun sparkled brightly. He couldn't put his finger on why, but a flood of excitement and anticipation rushed through his veins like a babbling brook.

Tenel Ka turned to him and quirked an eyebrow as the craft settled to the ground. "Yavin 4 does seem beautiful," she said, looking at him with a surprised expression, tossing red-gold braids away from her face. Jacen wondered if she had picked up on his emotions.

Jaina powered down the *Rock Dragon*'s engines. "I know what you mean. I feel the same. I'm looking forward to getting back to work on the reconstruction efforts around here—and even to all those tedious Jedi practice exercises."

Lowie gave a thoughtful rumble. With a whine and a blast of altitude-control jets, the *Millennium Falcon* landed beside them.

"When I saw the Great Temple from up in the sky, I felt relief," Tenel Ka continued. "From that altitude I could see no damage—only that the temple was still there, surrounded by all the jungle. Strange . . ."

"Maybe it's not so strange," Jaina said. "After seeing what the Death Star did to Alderaan, knowing that there's no way to repair that kind of destruction, I feel lucky that we all made it back here in one piece. Remember, the Death Star almost did the same thing to Yavin 4."

Lowie gave a short woof. "Oh, I agree, Master Lowbacca," Em Teedee said. "I have a definite preference for my planets and moons to be in one piece." Lowie finished the ship's shutdown procedures, and Jaina flicked the switch that extended the landing ramp. Han Solo and Chewbacca had already emerged from the *Millennium Falcon*.

"Look, there's Mom and Anakin," Jaina said, pointing out the front viewports, shading her eyes from the bright afternoon sunlight.

Watching his father dash down the ramp of the *Falcon* and swing Leia into his arms, Jacen suddenly remembered why he had felt so excited. Tonight, the entire Solo family would be together to celebrate his mother's birthday.

Jacen snatched open his crash webbing. He grinned a challenge at his sister. "Race you!" Before she even had a chance to say "What are you waiting for?" he scrambled out of his seat and headed for the exit.

That evening hundreds of torches flickered in the warm night air, decorating the Great Temple on Yavin 4. They burned at each corner on all levels of the pyramid, running in brilliant zigzagged columns up both sides of the stairways.

Jaina looked down the long wooden tables that had been used for her mother's birthday feast. The Jedi students and instructors, the New Republic engineers, and the few dignitaries who had come from Coruscant were just beginning to disperse, but Han, Luke, the twins, and Anakin would stay for a smaller, more private celebration, along with the family's closest friends, Chewbacca, Lowie, and Tenel Ka. Surrounded by her husband and children, Leia seemed unusually relaxed and contented.

"Happy birthday, Mom," Jaina said.

"I couldn't have asked for any more wonderful gift than to have my whole family with me," Leia answered. "It's such an unusual occurrence these days. And your father was very mysterious about this trip you all took."

Jaina suddenly wondered if she and Jacen had made the wrong choice for their mother's present. Would Leia be disappointed by the gift they had brought? Would it bring back too many painful memories about her lost home of Alderaan? What if it only saddened her?

Han put his arm around Leia. "The kids have a presentation to make. They got you something special."

Jaina glanced at Anakin, who quickly got the message. Her younger brother had always been perceptive. "I'll go first," he said.

Anakin flicked his fringe of straight brown hair away from his eyes and gently set a wrapped package the size of his fist on the table in front of his mother.

Leia carefully untied the strings and pulled back the glittering mesh that covered the gift. "Oh, Anakin. It's beautiful," she said, holding up a tiny stone replica of the Great Temple, a small ziggurat complete with the most meticulous details.

"I used the hologram as a pattern. I made this out of broken stone shards from the temple, pieces crushed too finely to use in the rebuilding. It's to remind you of what the temple will look like again, once we're all finished."

Jaina's throat tightened at the sight of the massive pyramid, intact again, if only in miniature. She nodded to Jacen, who reached beneath his seat, pulled out the gift that they had brought, and placed it on the table with a soft *thunk*.

Their mother gave them a grateful smile. "It's heavy—what is it, a rock?"

Jaina had prepared a speech to go with it, but suddenly she found she couldn't remember the words. She watched silently as her mother unwrapped the brightly colored cloth that held the shard of Alderaan. Lowbacca and Tenel Ka both looked on intently, in silence.

Leia studied it, ran her fingers over the metal's sparkling, faceted surface as if it crackled with electricity. "It's from Alderaan, isn't it?" she asked in a whisper.

"We wanted you to have a special piece of your home," Jaina said in a strained voice. "We know how much Alderaan meant to you, and that the Empire destroyed it—but in a sense, it's not really gone. We're children of Alderaan, too, because you passed on what you learned there to us. In a way, the spirit of Alderaan is very much alive."

"It's from the core of the planet," Jacen added. "From its heart."

Tears filled Leia's eyes. "Yes, I know it's from the heart," she said. "From Alderaan's, and from yours, as well. The heart is the one thing the Empire could never destroy. Those of us who survived—who weren't on the planet when it was blown up—carry the heart of Alderaan inside us. And we pass it on to our children."

"And speaking of children of Alderaan," Han said, looking at the twins, "your mom and Luke and I talked to Raynar this afternoon, let him know what's been going on with Boba Fett and Nolaa Tarkona and the bounty on his father's head."

"Han tells me that your friend Zekk offered to help us search for Bornan Thul," Leia said. "That's a brave thing for him to do. He must know there'll be danger."

"Oh, I'm sure he knows," Jaina said. "But he's changed. Everything changes, I guess. We just have to work hard to make the best of all those changes."

Suddenly she felt a pang of guilt over her selfishness. In her excitement at being reunited with her family, Jaina had completely forgotten about Raynar. At the moment, the young man had no hope of seeing his parents or any other relatives. He couldn't even be sure his father was still alive.

"Raynar could really use some good friends right now," Luke said. Her uncle's tone was mild, but Jaina heard the gentle rebuke in his words. She resolved to include the other boy more often in their daily activities. Glancing at Jacen, she saw that the same thoughts seemed to be running through his mind as well.

"This is a fact," Tenel Ka murmured. Lowbacca gave a thoughtful growl.

Leia raised a cup of juri juice. "To family," she said.

Han lifted his cup to touch hers. "And to appreciating what we've got—while we've got it."

"To family," echoed Jacen, Jaina, Anakin, Tenel Ka, and two enthusiastic Wookiees.

They all raised their cups and drank.

"KUAR, FIFTH PLANET orbiting a single sun in a star system of the same name," Tenel Ka said, reading her datapad while sitting in one of the passenger seats of the Hapan passenger shuttle. "Capable of sustaining human life, but apparently abandoned for some time. . . ."

"Does it say anything about particular cities or structures?" Jaina asked, craning her neck to look out the *Rock Dragon*'s cockpit windowport, peering down toward the vast planet below.

"Unfortunately, no," Tenel Ka said, consulting the datapad again.

Lowbacca rumbled a question about the level of technology that might remain on the planet.

"No data on the technology of Kuar's inhabitants. In fact," Tenel Ka said, holding up a finger to forestall the question

Jacen was about to ask, "I have nothing on the inhabitants whatsoever."

Jacen's face fell, then he brightened again. "What about wildlife? Interesting animal species, or plants?"

Tenel Ka shook her head grimly. "I've nothing more that is of any use to us, only the ramblings of historical scholars speculating about the original inhabitants, before the Mandalorians swept through.

"Em Teedee, have you additional data about Kuar?" Tenel Ka asked.

"Dear me, Mistress Tenel Ka, I'm afraid to say there's not much, really, aside from what you said. And the coordinates, of course—oh, here's something: Kuar's primary climate is semi-arid." The little droid made a sound like an aggrieved sigh. "I imagine that's not very useful at this point, is it?"

"We'll be able to speculate all we want for ourselves in a couple of minutes," Jaina said. "We're almost to the atmosphere. Okay, hit it, Lowie."

The young Wookiee flicked a few switches, and the ship nosed down toward the vast sky that provided only a thin blanket over the curved surface of Kuar.

Jaina flashed a conspiratorial grin at

her brother and Tenel Ka. "As I always say, show me—don't tell me."

Tenel Ka raised an eyebrow and turned to Jacen. "*Does* she always say that? I have not heard her."

Jacen merely shrugged. The *Rock Dragon* dove into the atmosphere.

The surface of Kuar was indeed semi-arid. The landscape alternated between dry dust and occasional rock formations or sand. It seemed as if the dust of time had sifted over the entire world. But the excitement of the adventure had overtaken Jacen, and he was impatient to know more about the mysterious place below. "Hey, what do the readings say?" he asked.

"Life forms," Jaina answered succinctly. "Quite a few, in fact."

Lowie gave a thoughtful purr. "Quite right, Master Lowbacca," Em Teedee said. "There's no telling yet whether the life forms are sentient or not."

A few thin clouds hung high in the atmosphere like worn and tattered lace, but they did little to obstruct Jacen's view. From this high up, the surface seemed relatively flat and featureless. "What about buildings?" he asked.

Lowie studied the readouts again and woofed a few times. "Most assuredly, Master Lowbacca. I'd agree that those aren't natural formations," Em Teedee said. "I'd hardly call them *buildings*, however. The structures are certainly old, but there's something odd about them—irregular, as if they're only half there."

"Ruins, perhaps?" Tenel Ka suggested.

"Quite probably," Em Teedee agreed.

"Why don't we just get closer and see?" Jacen asked impatiently.

Jaina sighed. "I was purposely staying high, hoping we'd spot a city or pick up a beacon of some sort to show us where the inhabited areas are. That's my guess for where Bornan Thul would have gone. I suppose you're right, though; we'll have to go down."

She took the *Rock Dragon* lower until they skimmed just two hundred meters above the surface. In most areas, the vegetation was fairly sparse. Rocky spikes and pillars and mounds jutted up from the landscape. Occasionally, Jacen saw what looked like a nest of some sort on one of the outcroppings. The color of the dirt, sand, and rock varied from cream, to gray, to pale

blue with purplish striations, to bright
ocher, to stark obsidian.

Lowie woofed and tapped the control
panel in front of him.

"Yep, I see it," Jaina said.

"What kind of structures?" Jacen asked.

"I'm afraid I can't say," Em Teedee replied. "They are approximately three kilometers ahead of us."

"There," Jaina said as she slowed the
Rock Dragon and dropped even lower to
get a good look. The thick wall that surrounded the small city atop a high, strate-
gic hill was broken in several places. Some
of the buildings seemed in good repair,
though others were cracked and crumbling.
A variety of furred and feathered creatures
bounded, scurried, or swooped from building
to building. Hundreds of yellow, six-legged
reptiles with curly tails clung to the sunny
side of every wall or turret.

"No people," Tenel Ka observed.

"Maybe they just abandoned this city for
some reason," Jacen said. He wished they
could stop to explore, so he could study
some of the strange creatures he had just
seen, but Jaina had already pulled the
Rock Dragon up and was looking for the

next city. They flew for hours across the surface of the planet, zig-zagging back and forth to cover more ground. They came upon a score of other ghost towns, fortresses, and villages in varying states of disrepair. None was inhabited; none had been disturbed in centuries.

And they found no clues to Bornan Thul's whereabouts, no evidence to show he, or anyone else, had been there.

Jacen was beginning to get nervous. He could see Jaina biting her lower lip. "Where *are* people when you need them?" he heard her mutter.

"You, um . . . you don't suppose," Jacen began, "that some war or virus or something could have killed everybody on Kuar, do you?"

Jaina darted him a startled look, as if she had not thought of this.

"No," Tenel Ka said simply.

"Rest assured, Master Jacen," Em Teedee chimed in, "all of the evidence indicates that the settlements we're seeing have been abandoned for hundreds—if not thousands—of years."

Jacen relaxed slightly. "What exactly are we looking for, anyway?"

"A landmark maybe?" Jaina said.

"An obvious meeting place," Tenel Ka suggested.

"Something that's easy to spot," Jaina said, "on an entire planet."

Lowie rumbled something about hangar bays.

"Or a good landing area," Jaina added. "Trust me, I'll know it when I see it." Jacen, Lowie, and Tenel Ka exchanged amused glances.

As it turned out, Jaina was right. It was nearly dawn before she saw a broad-based mesa that rose a kilometer above the cracked and dusty plain. As they drew closer, it became clear that the mesa, which was close to three kilometers wide, was not really a mesa. The majority of the mountain's flat top had collapsed into a deep crater, surrounded by an artificially broad, level rim, forming a gigantic natural arena.

Houses and tunnels and walkways and stairs had long ago been built into the sides of the crater. From the floor of the crater rose the ruins of a vast array of tall—or formerly tall—buildings. A webwork of rusty chains connected the tops of these buildings, like the design of some deranged insect. Jaina brought the *Rock*

Dragon in for a smooth landing on the spacious rim.

"Here we are," she said smugly. "Landmark. Easy to spot. Excellent landing area. This would be my guess." Lowie agreed enthusiastically.

"I'm showing no signs of airborne contaminants that would endanger the lives of humans or Wookiees," Em Teedee assured them. "The atmosphere is perfectly breathable."

"Everybody out, then," Jaina said. "Time to stretch our legs."

"Great," Jacen sighed, unbuckling his crash webbing. He was already thinking about what kinds of interesting creatures they might encounter.

"Now we begin the next stage of our search," Tenel Ka said. She followed Jacen down the shuttle's exit ramp. Jaina and Lowie tumbled after them, eager to move about after their long search.

Jacen ran to the edge of the crater and looked down at the patchwork of ancient buildings, chains, and walls dappled by shadows. "Could take a long time to look through all that," he said.

Lowie gave a negative growl. "Lowie's right. I think it would be more logical to start up here," Jaina said. "The best place to set down a ship would be somewhere along this rim." She made a sweeping gesture with one arm to indicate the wide ledge that encircled the crater.

After a brief consultation, the young Jedi Knights spread out from the rocky edge of the crater, spacing themselves to cover the most distance. They walked slowly around the rim, scanning the ground ahead and to each side for any sign of a recent disturbance in the ancient settled dust.

After several false alarms—which turned out to be nothing more than a gouge out of the rock, a shiny feather, or some animal droppings—Jacen, who was closest to the outer edge of the rim, saw something fluttering up ahead. Shading his eyes with one hand against the direct glare of the early morning sun, he ran forward. To his great disappointment, he found nothing more than a flat gray slab of rock, as large as one of the serving trays back at the Jedi academy. His sister, Lowie, and Tenel Ka dashed up beside him.

"What is it?" Jaina asked.

"Nothing, I guess," Jacen said. "I thought I saw something moving over here, fluttering. Maybe it was just a bird or a plume of dust, I don't know."

Tenel Ka bent low and circled the rock. "Ah. Aha," she said. She reached her hand beneath the edge and pulled. "Lowbacca, my friend?" she began, but before she could finish her request, Lowie had already lifted the slab of rock high overhead and then tossed it aside. Tenel Ka straightened. In her hand she held a long piece of cloth, a sash, sewn from alternating strips of yellow, purple, and orange fabric. "The colors of the House of Thul," she said matter-of-factly.

"Why, bless me," Em Teedee exclaimed. He was viewing the scene from a perspective that none of the others had. "Does the House of Thul also place inscriptions on its clothing?"

"Not that I've ever noticed," Jacen said, wondering what the little droid was getting at.

"May I see that?" Jaina asked. Tenel Ka handed her the sash. Jaina grasped the material with one hand near each end and stretched it out straight. She scanned the sash then flipped it over. "Look!"

Jacen moved closer. Sure enough, there

on the yellow band of material scratched in faint gray letters was a message.

"*Danger,*" it said. "*If I am caught, all humans in danger. Thul.*"

"Gracious me!" Em Teedee exclaimed. "I do hope Master Thul is safe."